Richard Carpenter's

ROBIN OF SHERWOOD

WHAT WAS LOST

by Elliot Thorpe

CONTENTS

PROLOGUE

The tiny village of Wellow went mostly unnoticed by the Sheriff of Bath and his officers.

The brook that coursed along the southernmost tip of the hamlet was forded at one point and the boy who was a very proud four years of age splashed and kicked at the cold water tumbling over his bare feet.

Nearby, his mother cradled a baby, still nursing but already full of spirit, as she called out to her son.

'Geoffrey, be careful that you don't slip!'

'No, mama,' he called, shielding his eyes from the chilly winter sun as he looked up at her sitting on the slope of grass. For a moment he stared downstream, thought about finding a rock to fling into the water, then dashed to his mother and kissed his sister on her tiny head. 'When will she be big enough to play with me?'

'She will be big enough soon! You'll need to show her how to walk first!'

'Can I show her now?'

'She doesn't know how to even crawl yet, my dearest!' Geoffrey's mother laughed, watching her boisterous son exaggerate his walking with strides as long as his little legs would allow. Esther dropped her gaze to the girl and stroked her head, reinforcing the love she had for her, the love Geoffrey had too, and the love her husband also carried in his heart. Their family was complete now and the baby she adored unconditionally was the gift they never thought they'd ever receive.

CHAPTER 1

The rain was cold, the wind needle-sharp in the merchant's eyes.

The storm had erupted quite suddenly, plunging the forest into near darkness, only punctuated with lightning that seemed to flash only to allow the hooded men to lunge out of the shadows. At each bolt, the figures got closer, felling each of the merchant's guards with terrifying ease. It was as if they were in tune with the storm, that the storm was somehow only raging with every slice of a sword, each thunderclap perfectly synchronised with every blow.

The merchant had been told that Sherwood Forest was alive with spirits but he was not a superstitious man, just one who saw sense in having men-at-arms with him. Not that his protection was much good now, lying as they were all around them.

The largest of the hooded men, his cowl tucked in at the neck into a large furred, sleeveless coat stomped towards the merchant, who was desperate to control his scared horse. The big man's beard bristled in the easing rain as he raised his quarterstaff.

'I'm armed!' the merchant sang out, his voice lost in the wind. 'I'm not afraid to use it!'

'What's your name?' the man growled.

'Jonas of Lytham,' the merchant replied, tremor to his voice. With his free hand he drew his sword. 'I told you I'm not afraid to use this!'

'I told you to stand your men down, Jonas of Lytham,' his large assailant hissed. 'I almost begged you. All we wanted was your money. Now their deaths are on you.'

'They were to… to protect me.'

'They didn't do much good then, did they, lad? Now...' The quarterstaff was at Jonas' throat. '...your money.'

Jonas's nerve broke then and he threw a bag onto the ground. It thudded with a heavy chink and the giant motioned to one of his companions.

'Much...'

A smaller man, probably still a boy by his clumsy movements, dashed to retrieve the bag.

'Much,' Jonas repeated almost under his breath. The merchant would surely remember that name if the opportunity arose to tell of the events that had happened here today.

Then, the leader of the hooded men offered two more.

'I'm John Little. This is Nasir,' said John, gesturing to a silent black-clad warrior by his side then to the forest around them, 'and this is Sherwood, our domain. You would be wise to remember that if you come this way again.'

It was then that Jonas went pale. There had only been three of them that had wiped out his entire group and he recognised those names from talk across the shires. 'You're Robin Hood's men... but it was said that you were all dead.'

'Wishful thinking,' replied John. 'Now be on your way, lad.'

Jonas didn't need telling twice and clumsily mounted his horse, wet boots slipping in the stirrups. Nasir slapped the horse's rump and it whinnied in indignation, galloping off into the trees.

A beam of sunlight broke through the gloom as Much handed John the large purse. John noticed the boy's worried expression.

'Trouble?' he asked.

'It's what the merchant said, John. Reckon it's true?'

'What do you mean?'

'He thought we were all dead.'

'Just talk, lad,' John responded. 'Just talk. Although it certainly feels different now. Like a part of us has died.'

'We'll be alright, won't we, John?'

'We'll be alright,' the big man assured him.

'But there is a question,' Nasir suddenly said.

Much and John turned to look at him, glancing at each other.

'Spit it out,' said John.

'Why would a merchant need seven men-at-arms to protect him and just one bag of gold?'

The answer didn't come then and it was still playing on their minds by the time they had returned to the village of Wickham.

The Palace of Winchester was surrounded on all sides by grazing land, open and undeterred by the constant flow of traders, soldiers returning from or heading out to battle and holy men summoned by the Royal Court.

There were rumours afoot of the King making a permanent court at Westminster but nothing was certain and John's movements were always close to his chest. If the change *was* to be made, it would ultimately make little difference to the person on the street, those in the towns, in the villages and on the farms. For the time being, the Court would remain almost nomadic in its functionality and indeed the King had only just left the Palace, Canterbury the next destination unfortunate enough to receive his presence.

He'd left behind a prisoner, one who was personally known to him and one who had become something of a thorn in his side these last few months. There was a great delight in leaving such a wretch where he was but the King, for all his bluster and seething rages, still had to obey the law to some extent, his powers stunted even further by the connections to the church his prisoner had. Family was strong and sometimes a hindrance and the brothers de Rainault were no different. John couldn't abide the sanctimonious Abbot Hugo and was glad to leave rather than be in his perfumed Godly presence.

He knew why the Abbot had arrived and what was about to take place in the putrid gloom of a dungeon cell so many feet below the Palace and he was relieved not to be a part of it.

Abbot Hugo too was glad that the King wasn't in residence and it gave confidence to his gait as he approached the last of the tiny cells at the end of a long, narrow corridor, one where the darkness was weakly punctuated with irregularly-placed flaming torches.

He halted at the heavy, wooden door and motioned for the guard to open it. With some effort, warped by damp and disuse, it was unbolted and wrenched open. What light there was from the torches that burned within the corridor spilled in and as weak as it was, it was too much for the incumbent prisoner who cowered, his eyes erupting in pain. It had been months since anyone had shown an interest in him let alone actually opened the door.

Hugo took a step forwards, the fetid atmosphere assaulting his nose.

'God's teeth, this place stinks. You stink, Robert.'

Robert de Rainault, the once proud and omnipotent Sheriff of Nottingham, who had been reduced to a bedraggled, shaggy-bearded unfortunate, forced to eat slop from wooden bowls passed to him through a slit in the door and throw his own effluence into the corner of the tiny cell, couldn't believe his ears. He coughed and spluttered as he tried to speak, Hugo leaning in and passing him a goblet of clean water.

'Easy, brother,' Hugo said as Robert gulped down the nectar.

'Hu… Hugo?' Robert said eventually, almost unwilling to accept this wasn't yet another fever induced dream.

'Yes, Robert!'

'I never… never thought I'd see you again.'

The Abbot, in his fine clerical robes, looked at his filth encrusted brother, a shadow of his former self.

'Perseverance runs in the family, brother. I'm surprised you gave up so easily.'

'Shut the door!' Robert shielded his eyes as he looked up at Hugo. 'Shut it! Please!'

'No, Robert,' came the firm reply. 'If you want to walk out of here, you will have to get used to the light.'

'What are you saying?'

'Do you need me to spell it out? We're leaving here.'

Robert shied away again, tears of relief mixing with the brightness. 'Where… where to?'

'Where do you think?'

'Your footsteps. I recognised them. They might have been mine when I used to walk the… the corridors of Nottingham castle.' *But that was another life, when I had been the Sheriff.*

Hugo stepped back outside the cell for a moment and gestured to the two monks who had travelled with him. As much as he loved his brother he wasn't about to touch him.

The monks steadied Robert to his feet and helped him shuffle out of the cramped hovel that had been his home for so long, and led him down along the corridor and to the wider, lighter area where the guards usually sat. A space had been cleared for them. It was clear he was in pain, wincing with every step and he'd not sat down on a chair in months. That very act seemed to cause him so much discomfort that Hugo ordered the monks to lower him to the floor, where Robert sat in relief.

'I'd given up hope, Hugo,' he breathed.

'I didn't. Almost a year of petitioning and a vast amount of money, but finally, here we are,' was the Abbot's reply.

The monks peeled away the encrusted rags over Robert's thin frame, careful not to injure him. Bathing would need to wait until they were away from this place but in the meantime, he was cleansed with damp cloths and scented with herbs.

'I'm grateful to you Hugo. For all you've done. I'll make it up to you.'

Before Hugo's very eyes, his brother was slowly returning: the months of beard growth cut and shaved away, lank hair clipped tidy to above his neckline.

'There's no need, brother. It was your money after all.'

'What!' de Rainault spluttered, a flash of the old anger there in an instant.

'What else could I do, Robert? You're my brother and it was my duty to use whatever monies you had to get you out,' said the Abbot. 'Besides, I couldn't waste Church coffers.'

Robert began to feel his eye twitch. 'So if I had no money, I would have rotted in there?'

'I'll be honest with you, brother, the King has bled you dry. I don't really blame him after that embarrassment with the golem-thing. And that's the good news.'

Robert ate greedily at the bowl of bread and cold meats one of the monks brought into the chamber. He did not ever want to be reminded of the trickery the bedevilled Gulnar had played on them all. 'The good news?'

'Yes. You could be dead or be off prosecuting the King's wars in France. That's where Gisburne is.'

'Gisburne? Officially in the King's employ?' sneered Robert. 'He will be unbearably smug. Let's hope he catches gangrene from a random stabbing.'

There was no love lost between Robert and his former steward, Sir Guy.

'The name de Rainault was all but banned from being mentioned. I had to use considerable Church muscle to be able to broach the subject of a petition and release.'

'As long as you use my money, of course.'

'Of course.'

'How dare he,' de Rainault whispered. 'I'll make him pay!"

'Wait until you get your strength back before you start up your own little crusade, brother.'

'I'm not talking about King John.'

Hugo sighed. 'I know you're not.'

'There is one man who is truly responsible for all of this.' Robert paused for a moment, swigging at the wine his stomach seemed to be able to cope with now. His eyes widened. 'Unless of course...'

'No such luck, Robert. Robin Hood is still alive as far as is known.'

'Well,' Robert sighed, returning to his small feast, 'I wouldn't have believed you anyway. But what do you mean: as far as is known?'

'Huntington disappeared. A year ago? Maybe more. It's hard to tell. Very little was heard.'

'And what of his men?'

'I sent a young man, a merchant, into Sherwood with a bag of coins to see if he'd come back out again.'

'How wonderfully twisted of you, Hugo. Did he make it?' Robert threw the chicken leg into the bowl and drank some more wine. 'Don't keep me in suspense!'

'First things first. There is more important news at hand, news that concerns Sister Marion of Halstead.'

'Who the devil is Sister Marion of Halstead?' Robert spat.

'Ah, yes,' Hugo said, coughing, 'You wouldn't know. The Maid Marion, she of Leaford, is married to the Church now.'

'I can only imagine that wedding day,' Robert laughed. 'What of her?'

Hugo leaned in close and began to tell his brother.

CHAPTER 2

Robin of Sherwood knew Marion was lost to him and he could not begin to think otherwise without the drink to help.

She was always in his thoughts, there at the periphery when he didn't want her to be or walking towards him from out of the trees, his dreams as lucid as any waking moment. He longed for the day when she was no longer just a dream but the memories coursed through his addled brain. And they weren't always solely about her: Adam Bell, the disgraced outlaw; the brutal nobleman Owen of Clun; the Baron de Belleme who… no… no, that was another memory of another man's; Herne the Hunter, his presence slicing through all the broken and tattered thoughts and always there was Marion, calling to him, beckoning. Then he would awaken, skin clammy and hair plastered to his forehead and neck, breathing shallow and fast.

This morning was no different and he slumped back down in the hay, the wind outside rattling the barn door. He was vaguely aware of an old maid in the corner of the barn milking a cow, the animal snorting and shuffling as it filled the wooden bucket. Robin nodded off again, unaware that the woman had been staring at him these past few moments. Neither did he hear the great door swing open, the hay around where he was lying swirling up in the string breeze.

***

Little John, wet through from the brewing storm, purposely allowed the door to slam shut.

'Robin!' he called out, the evidence of the previous night's drinking plain to see. 'Robin!'

'Quietly, boy! You'll turn milk sour,' the woman growled, patting her cow on its hind quarters. 'There, my beauty. You stay calm now.'

John didn't answer her but leaned in close to his sleeping friend. How much ale had he drank last night? 'Hey, Robin,' he called, more softly this time, but still loud enough to warrant a glare from the maid.

Robin still did not respond so John shook him, gently at first, then with more vigour. Robin sat up, startled, angry, hand reaching out around him for a sword he didn't have.

'Oh, it's you, John.' Robin put his head in his hands. It hurt abominably. 'What time is it?'

As Robin took a moment to get his wits, John stood over him. 'Still early.'

'And raining,' Robin noted.

'Aye. The storm broke again before we could get back.'

'You've been hunting?' Robin asked.

'In a manner of speaking. There are more gentry than ever in the forest these days. We can't keep up with them all. There's not enough of us.'

'There's no Sheriff, no one to stop them.'

'No one to stop them? Robin, it used to be us that stopped them. Remember?'

'I remember,' Robin breathed, slumping back down into the hay. 'Of course I remember.'

John stepped back and shook his head. It seemed it would take a miracle to get Robin back on his feet, to care again. He couldn't help but wonder if Meg was right. 'When the rain stops, we could get back out, if you fancy it?' John ventured hopefully.

A grunt was the response John got, so he tried again. But Robin wasn't listening, instead pretending to be asleep once more.

The barn door rattled again and John turned, ready to cross to it to close it firmly. But Meg was standing outside, a shawl over her shoulders and arms, looking intently at the stilted exchange between the two old friends. She was the last person John wanted to see and he tried to ignore her defiant expression and stayed where he was.

'I was just thinking about you,' he said.

Meg looked past John to the blonde-and-Lincoln-Green heap on the floor.

'John…' murmured the heap.

John turned back to Robin and knelt. 'Yes, lad?'

'Would you do something for me?'

'Anything,' his loyal lieutenant replied.

'Get out and leave me alone,' came the blunt request. Robin turned over and buried his face in the straw, ignoring the loose chaff that was tickling his eyelashes and wanting nothing more than to get back to sleep.

John stood, angry and annoyed.

He knew Robin had been hurting for a long time but surely there was only so much patience any of them could have?

Meg standing without, the rain lashing across her face, was becoming more agitated and as John tried to walk away, she stepped in front of him.

'Are you just going to ignore me, John?'

'What do you want me to say? That you're right? That the point you've been trying to make this past year or so has been proved right?'

Robin Hood, the legend, and in many ways, the man, was dead. What was left was a husk. Oblivious. Withdrawn. Drunk.

'If you're saying that,' Meg replied tartly, 'then you must think it true, too.'

'But I don't think I'm… I don't know what to think…' John shook his shaggy mane. 'It's been hard on all of us.'

'Has it? Has it really? And why is that, John?'

John began walking away and Meg turned to draw level with him, heading back to the main section of the village.

'Don't ignore me!' Meg grabbed John's elbow but he spun, rage in his eyes. She drew back, shocked. Then she stood fast once more in front of him. He had no choice but to stop. 'Don't treat me like that. Who do you think you are?'

'I'm sorry, Meg. It's just that everything has changed.'

'You all want to be back in Sherwood playing cat and mouse with the Sheriff of Nottingham. But there is no sheriff anymore! The fight is over.' She pulled the shawl tighter around her shoulders, her hair plastered in the rain. 'Why can't you see that if we are to have a future, then we have to leave Wickham?'

'You ask too much.'

'Do I?'

'I ask the man I love to think about how I feel and he says it's too much? This is torture. For both of us.'

John nodded but his answer to her was always the same: Robin was Herne's son.

'And?' asked Meg.

'And he's my friend. He needs my help, all our help. I'm not about to abandon him.'

'Like Herne has abandoned him?'

'That's not fair.'

'It's not?'

'No. He is my friend. I will not leave him. I will not.'

'*She* did.'

That struck hard in John's gut. 'Careful,' he warned her.

'Or what, John? It's been long enough for you to see he's not the same. He never will be,' Meg persisted.

'All the more reason then not to forget what he has been, to you, to me, to all of us,' exclaimed John.

'*Has been* is right,' was Meg's angry response.

'Come with me.' John took her hand and led her to a small outhouse, normally where the manure was kept. Hidden in a trough, under the dirt, was the bag of coins they had taken from Jonas the merchant. 'Let me remind you of something.'

John poured the contents out onto the floor.

'Am I supposed to be impressed?'

There was a time when Wickham welcomed them, but now, they were buying time. Time which was becoming expensive in so many ways.

'It's this money that Robin brings to us all.'

'Robin? You got hold of this while he snored liked a sow. He did nothing.' Meg folded her arms and glared at the spoils, frowned and looked at them more closely. 'John…'

'Meg, I don't want to argue.'

'No, John. Look!' Meg bent down and scooped up a handful of the coins. Mixed in with the silver were thin wooden discs, faded and bleached. 'You can't even rob a merchant right. You've all been had!'

'What the hell?' John grabbed a large handful himself and examined them closely. It was true: over half of the bulging purse was made up of these wooden fakes, the same size and thickness as the silver coins.

***

'How did we not realise?' John asked Nasir as they sat in Edward's lodgings, the storm outside seemingly relentless. 'How could we be so stupid?'

Edward was the head of the village and for years had been a friend and supporter of Robin and his men so it was natural that they found themselves around the fire drinking mead with him. John was disturbed that they had been fooled so easily. The wooden coins were strewn across the table.

'I knew there was something not right about the merchant,' growled Nasir.

'Perhaps he had been robbed by someone else? Didn't want to be in trouble for having less than he started with?' suggested Edward.

'A worthy explanation but no, Nasir is right. A merchant with one bag of coins, hoax ones at that, with so many armed men? It doesn't make sense.'

'A trap,' Nasir breathed.

'But to what end? They did not put up much of a fight, you said, John.'

'They didn't, Edward. It was like they were expendable simply for the benefit of us taking the merchant's money.'

'Did you recognise the merchant, this Jonas?' Edward asked.

'I have not seen him before,' qualified Nasir.

'Nor me,' added Much. 'We used to know all the tax collectors and the rich men that went through Sherwood. Back in the old days.'

'He was young,' said John. 'Perhaps we're just getting too old. When the money lenders and the tax officers are our juniors, what does that make us?'

'You're not past it yet, John!' exclaimed Edward. 'I always wanted to join you and the others, Tuck, Scarlet, Marion… but it never quite happened. As the seasons went on I always hoped, but Robin found a way to keep me here.'

The room fell silent for a while as those names hung heavy in the air. Names of friends gone. Then John placed a great palm on Edward's shoulder.

'He was keeping you alive. You were always our safe house. You still are! You are more use to us here than with us in Sherwood. We couldn't have done it without you.'

Much nodded, playing with the fake money. 'Should we tell Robin?'

'Robin doesn't need to know, lad,' replied John.

'But he's our leader,' responded Much, sorrow in his voice.

None of them would ever consciously want to deceive Robin, but with him spending his waking days downing ale, John and Nasir had taken control of things. It was the way it had to be until Robin was back on his feet again and Much always kept the hope in his heart that it would happen one day soon.

'Do you think it was a one-off?' asked Edward.

'A lure? I don't like to think so, but you may be right.' John gathered the wooden coins up and threw them in the fire, retaining one as a keepsake, a reminder that they were perhaps beginning to lose sight of their purpose.

***

Dawn was breaking over the land and the storm had abated for now, just a strong wind whistling through the corridors and battlements of Nottingham Castle.

In his chambers, Robert de Rainault shuffled to his bed, his weakened state frustrating him as much as causing fatigue during even the easiest of formal engagements.

Word of his return office has been surprisingly slow and that was the way he preferred it: he hoped that the news hadn't yet filtered out to the villages or into forest itself. He needed to get his strength back and fast before re-engaging the infamous Sherwood outlaws.

Just as he settled his head on his pillow after a disturbed night, a rapping came at his thick oak door. 'Oh, go away!' he growled. There would be time for audiences later. Now he needed to sleep.

But the knocking came again and the Sheriff didn't have the strength to argue.

The door creaked open and Hugo entered, bringing with him a young man, nervous, but eyes alert and watching.

'Brother,' Hugo began. 'This cannot wait.'

'God's curse, Hugo,' Robert spat, pulling his bed clothes over his thin frame. 'Is there no peace for me?'

'I thought your months in solitary would make you eager for company,' derided his brother.

'Far from it, Hugo. It was time well-spent to think about how I can be rid of Robin Hood once and for all.'

'Then you will enjoy this,' Hugo chuckled, waving the man forward. 'Tell my Lord Sheriff what you told me.'

Robert glared at the stranger, days' growth of stubble on his face, but young all the same.

'My name is Jonas of Lytham,' Jonas said, voice breaking.

'"My name is Jonas of Lytham, *my Lord*",' Hugo said with venom. 'Show some respect.'.

'Yes, of course, sorry, my Lord… my Lords,' Jonas said.

'What do you want you pitiful boy?' asked Robert. 'I have had quite enough already. It's bad enough having to receive you in my private chambers without you quivering all over the place. Get on with it or get out.'

'My Lord,' Jonas began, glancing between the de Rainault brothers, 'I have news of Robin Hood.'

Robert sat up, forgetting he was unwell, and immediately regretted it. But he wasn't about to miss this. 'Well? Speak up!'

'The Abbot Hugo sent me into Sherwood with a bag of coins.'

'And some men at arms,' added Hugo.

'Yes, and some men at arms.'

'And he was ambushed by Robin Hood!'

'It wasn't Robin Hood himself,' Jonas said, daring to correct the Abbot. 'I never saw Robin Hood.'

'Then who was it?' asked de Rainault, grabbing a goblet of wine and downing it to help deal with the shooting pains in his back.

'The leader said he was John. He was with Nasir and the miller's son.'

'And who else? Scatlock? The friar?' pressed Robert.

'No, my Lord, just the three of them.'

'Just the three…' pondered Robert. 'And you're sure about this? The others weren't in hiding?'

'No, my Lord.'

'Three of them, Robert!' said Hugo. 'They're done for!'

'They killed all of my men,' Jonas pointed out.

'Savages,' Robert seethed. 'And who authorised you to take these guards with you? Was it you. Hugo?'

'It seemed unfair to send him in alone, Robert. I agreed when he asked me.'

Robert leaned over to grab a goblet and threw it down when he found it empty. 'Your ruse obviously worked though. The outlaws clearly assumed this boy here was carrying more than he was if he needed such protection.'

Hugo explained the deception with the wooden coins and Robert laughed, finding this highly amusing. But he strained his chest and sagged back onto his bed, coughing and wheezing.

'But it has brought other worms to the surface,' Hugo added, watching his brother struggle to catch his breath. His eyes flicked to Jonas. 'Leave us.'

After a while, Robert was settled again, having moved towards the burning fireplace. He poured himself a fresh goblet of wine, the discarded one having rolled under his bed, and stared at the flames.

'The story is everywhere, brother,' Hugo said now they were alone.

'And what story would that be?' asked Robert, knowing full well what Hugo was referring to.

The Abbot was in no mood for his brother being obtuse. There was only one story on people's lips, that the Sheriff had been robbed some days ago, and by his own men, the ones responsible for the shire's tax collections making it to the castle treasury safely.

'A bit of a disaster, wouldn't you say, Hugo? Who knows if there is truth in these things, eh? It's a good job I have a plan,' Robert de Rainault said, his mind having been working steadily since Hugo told him about Sister Marion.

'You know where I stand,' Hugo replied.

'I believe I do,' said the Sheriff.

If there was any doubt in the Abbot's mind of his brother's return to form, it was gone in a flash. Robert may have aged during his time in the goal, may have become so emaciated that it would take weeks to fully get back to his previous level of health, but Hugo could see the determination to succeed was still there.

As brothers, they were better off together and Hugo was ready to play his part.

CHAPTER 3

Springtime in Somerset usually meant bright days and blue skies framing the budding flowers and blossom on the trees, but the storm that had swamped the much of the country during the winter months was, while not as intense, still making life difficult for man, beast and nature alike.

Geoffrey of Wellow was out in one of the lower fields of the village overseeing the sowing of the new crops. The ground was sodden and added hours to the working day but he daren't stop in case the dark clouds burst again. And so the villagers worked until dusk, until they could no longer clearly see the ground before them, eventually trudging home under the watchful gaze of the moon.

Esther was glad to see her husband, hugging him tightly, not caring about the mud caked on his clothes and arms.

'Hard work, that was,' he said, pulling his leather boots off, feet damp and aching. 'Did they settle easy?'

Esther nodded and spooned some broth into a bowl for him. 'She took a while but once I took her out of her cot, she was fine.'

Geoffrey looked over to their baby who was sleeping soundly in their bed. 'I hope she doesn't make a habit of this. She should be in her own cot,' he smiled. 'And the boy?'

'He was desperate to stay up until you came home but he feel asleep not long ago.'

Their son, named after his father, was asleep by the fire. Geoffrey stroked his son's head and started tucking into his meal. 'The boy needs to grow big and strong if this weather doesn't turn. I've never known anything like it.'

'It won't be long until he's out there with you. He already wants to be.'

'P'raps I can teach him about lambing next year, eh?'

'Little Geoffrey is so full of life. I hope he doesn't want to go and fight one day.'

There was always a battle or a skirmish going on somewhere on the continent and often those from the abbey would come down into the villages, full of religious fervour to entice the young men away to war.

'Who knows, my love,' the senior Geoffrey said through mouthfuls, stopping for a while and staring at the contents of his bowl.

'What's wrong? Food taste bad?'

'Eh? What's that?' Geoffrey was distracted. His aching shoulders slumped, his expression fallen and lips surrounded by a few days' beard growth pursed. 'No, no, sorry. It's really lovely. As always.'

'What is it then?' Esther sat next to her husband. 'Tired?'

'Yes… yes, that's it. I'm tired,' he shrugged and continued eating. Then he stopped again and put the bowl and ladle down on the little rickety wooden stool by their bed. 'It's them crops. I don't think they'll yield. It's just too damn wet.'

'There's nothing you can do, though. If you didn't sow them then we'd have nothing come summer. At least we might get a chance.'

'Then there's the lambs. Six stillborns already. It's like we're cursed.'

'Oh, don't go saying things like that, Geoffrey,' Esther said, shuddering and leaning into her husband's arms.

'I'm sorry, my love. I was talking to the head of Twinhoe the other day. He was saying too about how they're struggling. It's not just us. It's everywhere. All the villages. Perhaps we were wrong to… y'know…' His voice trailed off as he looked at the baby.

'Geoffrey!' Esther snapped, standing and taking the bowl from the stool. 'I'll not have that talk in my home! That baby was a gift from Mother Nature herself and you'll not say otherwise. She's ours to raise, to look after. And we will damn well do that no matter what the stupid rain outside says we can't do.'

Geoffrey shook his head. 'I'm sorry, Esther, I didn't mean that.'

Esther tried to ignore him as he stood and moved to her side, his rough hands stroking her auburn hair, but she turned to him and sighed. 'It will all be right, Geoffrey, you'll se—'

'Geoffrey!' came a cry as the door to their home burst open. 'Geoffrey! You need to come quickly!'

In the doorway was one of the elder villagers, panting and gesturing for Geoffrey to go with him.

'Good grief, Roy, what is the matter?'

Esther told both men to be quiet through fear of waking the children so Geoffrey grabbed a cloak and hurried outside, pulling the door shut.

'Geoffrey, forgive me for disturbing your peace but our lookout has seen riders coming from the north.'

'Riders? Show me…' This was not something usually of concern. Wellow was oftentimes a place to stop before travellers found passage to Wales from Bristol but these were coming from the other direction and Roy seemed unnaturally worried. They hurried to the Twinhoe road. 'What makes these riders different?'

'Because they were seen in Midford and they ransacked most of the village.'

'What of Twinhoe?'

'I don't know, but look at them…'

Roy pointed and Geoffrey followed his indicating finger. The moonlight made it difficult to see but Geoffrey determined there were at least twelve horses galloping at speed towards them, drawn swords glinting in the gloom. 'Weapons out? That means they're her for trouble. Take the children, get them to the Long Barrow. They'll be safe there. Do it quietly.'

'What will you do?' asked Roy.

'I'm going to take the able-bodied, form a party and try to hold them off.'

***

'No! I won't go! They're asleep!'

Esther was stubborn and forthright, a combination that made it difficult for her to be reasoned with sometimes. Geoffrey loved her for it but today it was frustrating.

'Please, my wife,' he hissed. 'The others are taking refuge. We don't know what they want but we need to keep everyone safe. Roy is instructing the others to do the same.'

Indignant and grumbling, she stirred the boy and wrapped the baby in swaddling, who didn't wake even as little Geoffrey started crying, his sleep disturbed.

From under the bed, the senior Geoffrey pulled an axe, weighing it in his hands and pushed his family out into the dark and across the open land, past the other homes and into the channel of villagers heading towards the empty barrow on the edge of the woods.

But looming up from out of the night came a horse, whinnying and stomping, nostrils flaring. It scattered the villagers who began to scream and cry out in fear, only to be rounded up by more horses.

The riders wore black chainmail over dark clothing. A crest was painted on some of the riders' shields but the half-light made it difficult to determine what it represented. One of the strangers, the leader, brought his horse into the middle of the village, sword raised.

'Silence! Silence all of you!'

The throng took a few more commands to settle, partly delivered by some blows to a number of the villagers.

'What do you want?' called Geoffrey. 'We have nothing here for you.'

The leader shouted Geoffrey down, his voice laced with a foreign accent. 'That is not for you to determine. Are you the head of the village?'

'Yes. Yes, I am,' Geoffrey replied defiantly, axe behind his back and ready to be swung.

'Good. Then it is you I need to speak with.' The leader dismounted and Geoffrey was taken aback as to how tall he was, at least two or three heads higher than he. 'My name is Mouchard. You will be advised to remember it out of respect. We are your masters here, now.'

'The Sheriff of Bath is our master, sir,' replied Geoffrey, something that was met with a strike across his face. But he stood firm, his face stinging and his ears ringing. 'Have you his authority to be here?'

'I do not need your sheriff's permission. I am here on my own business.' Mouchard circled Geoffrey, making it impossible for the smaller man to hide the axe. Mouchard took it, examining it closely. Geoffrey cursed under his breath. 'Did you intend to use this on me?'

'Surely you can understand my need to protect my village?'

Mouchard nodded. 'Yes, I would do the same. But I would not allow my village to be invaded so easily!'

This led to peals of laughter from the strangers, some of whom had dismounted now and were prowling through the scared villagers.

'What do you want from us?' Geoffrey was determined to stand his ground.

Mouchard ignored him and instead spun, addressing the congregation. 'Which of you is Esther?'

'We have no one by that name here. You are clearly mistaken,' was Geoffrey's reply, at which Mouchard launched the axe clear across the group to kill one of the women, his aim true and final. More screams rose up and some of the children began sobbing hysterically.

'You pig!' Geoffrey spat, launching himself at Mouchard.

'I do hope that was not Esther,' the man said coolly.

'Leave us alone!' Geoffrey demanded through gritted teeth, moving to the fallen villager and obscuring her fatal wound from the others with his cloak. 'Leave us and go.'

Again, Mouchard ignored him and again Mouchard asked the question. No one spoke up.

'Bring me another axe,' he said. 'It is clear these people are backwards.'

'No! Enough!' Geoffrey cried.

'Then another dies.'

Silence fell across the field, none of the villagers sure about what to do next. They were all looking to Geoffrey for guidance but he looked as helpless as the rest. Then one of them spoke up and Geoffrey's heart sank.

'I'm Esther,' said Esther.

'What—'

But Mouchard cut Geoffrey off. 'Are you indeed? Who can vouch that this is the woman Esther?' None of the villagers replied but Mouchard saw a fleeting expression of fear and anger across Geoffrey's face. 'You… you are gnashing your teeth. I can see your jaw clenching. It is that this woman is Esther?'

Geoffrey looked straight ahead, determined not to reveal who the woman was.

'I am Esther. Now leave the others be.'

Geoffrey shot his wife a glance but it was enough to give Mouchard the confirmation he needed.

'Your wife is Esther, yes?' Mouchard moved his face uncomfortably close to Geoffrey's. 'Yes?'

'What… what do you want with her?'

'I am lonely. I… *we*… have travelled far. Can you not see that keeping all these women to yourself is selfish?' Mouchard's expression never wavered, his eyes locked onto Geoffrey's. Then he began to laugh. 'You English! You have no sense of humour!'

The other riders joined in, unnerving the villagers even further. No one dared question if they really were joking or if they did intend to take Esther and the other women to do with them what they pleased.

'Where is your baby?' Mouchard asked, his laugh dropping as quickly as it had arisen.

This took both Geoffrey and Esther aback. In the dash towards the barrow, Esther had put the children under the care of one of the other mothers. The woman was trembling at the rear of the group, little Geoffrey at her feet and Esther's swaddled baby in her arms. Why would this man be interested in their baby? Then Geoffrey and Esther looked at each other. How could this stranger possibly know..?

One of the riders snatched the baby from the woman's arms.

'My Lord!' he called as the baby began to cry.

'Take the woman, too!' Mouchard commanded.

Amid more screams, the mercenaries moved to pull Esther and her crying baby towards a waiting cart. As they did, Geoffrey tried in vain to stop them but was knocked to the ground, fire in his eyes and panic as his wife and baby were bundled onto the cart.

'If there is any resistance, we will burn your village to nothing! Wellow will be erased from existence!'

One of the riders, a burly gruff individual, his English accent contrasting against the European dialect of his companions, moved to speak to Mouchard. 'Do we need to do this?'

Mouchard looked the mercenary up and down, recognising him even under the bulky helmet as one who never seemed settled in the group. 'What does it look like? Business,' was Mouchard's reply.

'Taking peasants from villages isn't something I joined up to do.'

'I agree,' Mouchard nodded as the other man removed his helmet, revealing a face that Geoffrey was sure he had seen before. 'There is treasure here.' Noting the confusion on the mercenary's face, he looked across at Esther and her child. "They will make us very rich, which is why you're being entrusted with the mission to escort them back to Bertrand. In the meantime, I will take the rest of the men. We all have a part to play in this and soon you will understand.'

Now Mouchard turned his attention back to Geoffrey who had found his courage again, perhaps because of this other mercenary's challenge.

'Where are you taking them?'

'Your wife and child,' Mouchard began, enjoying seeing Geoffrey become more agitated, 'they will come to no harm. My orders are quite specific.'

'What of the rest of us?'

'Like I said, any of you resist, you will burn. Do you understand?'

The cart was already moving off before Geoffrey had any chance to object. 'It seems I have little choice,' he breathed, watching Esther soothe their baby, tears on her cheeks splashing onto the little one's forehead.

'I can see why they made you head of the village. You might not be wise, perhaps, but you are sensible.' Mouchard pulled his horse firm and mounted. 'Remain so and all will be well.'

With a cry in a language Geoffrey was sure was French, Mouchard rallied his riders together and they all moved out with their prisoners, fading into the darkness as quickly as they had emerged.

The villagers watched them go in stunned and fearful silence before heading back to their beds, although none of them could ever begin to think about sleeping that night.

***

'You're a long way from your jurisdiction, Sheriff,' Sister Marion had said when the de Rainault brothers were granted access to the grounds of Halstead Abbey.

It had been a long ride and Robert had just about come to the end of his patience, Hugo also relieved to have arrived, mainly to be free of his brother's grumblings. In fairness, though, this had been the first major journey Robert had been physically able to tolerate since returning to his duties and it hadn't been easy for him. Even now, as they walked slowly around the cloisters, it was noticeable that his gait was laced with pain.

The warm sun glinted through the few apple trees in the middle of the rectangle of grass and Marion smiled and said good morning to a nun who was tending the trees' branches as she brought the tour to a halt.

'This is not easy, my Lord Sheriff.'

'You have been granted special dispensation by the Mother Superior. I have seen to that,' Hugo pointed out.

'But nevertheless...' Marion sighed. This had not been a comfortable meeting and she had not been pleased to see the two men.

'What my brother is telling you,' the Sheriff said, 'is that you have no need to worry about your ecclesiastical duties, for as long as necessary.'

The emphasis and tone was not lost on Marion and she knew by the distasteful look in his eyes that the Sheriff did not take her decision to join the nunnery seriously.

'There is much at stake here,' nodded Hugo.

'Do you understand exactly what?' added the Sheriff.

'You and the Abbot have made it very clear,' she finally said, leading them towards the great wooden door that led to the outside world. 'But what you're asking is difficult.'

'Really?' questioned the Sheriff. 'Is that so?'

'You have an obligation to the church,' the Abbot added. 'Not to mention my turning a blind eye to your refuge within the order.'

'My refuge?' she asked, stopping at the door. 'Is this what you think this is? That I'm hiding?'

'Well aren't you?' the Sheriff pushed. 'An outlaw running rife throughout Sherwood with a group of cut-throat peasant men who suddenly has the calling… thereby absolving her of any villainous wrong-doing?'

'Robin was the son of an Earl, don't forget,' Marion challenged.

'Oh, I've not forgotten!' the Sheriff replied. 'Far from it. But that still doesn't change the fact that you are hiding from justice.'

'*Norman* justice,' she said.

'What other kind of justice is there, Sister Marion?' questioned Hugo.

Marion looked up at her tormentors, finally resigned to what she was required to do. 'I will do what you ask,' she said softly.

'See, Hugo? I told you she would relent.'

'But what if I fail?'

'That's obvious,' Hugo said, but the Sheriff was far more blunt.

'If you fail, Sister Marion, then a huge part of your life will be over. Is that clear? Well… *is it*?'

'Yes, my Lord Sheriff. Abundantly.'

CHAPTER 4

Of all the threats he had faced, this one scared Little John the most because of what it might force him to do. The angry mob before him were the villagers of Wickham, people he had no desire to hurt. He roared at them to stay back as he brought his quarterstaff up. By his side, Nasir and Much stood ready.

Edward was calling for quiet, to bring some order back, but no one was listening. He turned to John: 'Perhaps it's for the best of you make for the forest… for now.'

Much was getting upset. He considered Wickham his home after Sherwood. 'Why should we, John?'

'We don't have to, lad,' John replied, then addressed the mob: 'You were all quick to ask for our help when you needed it, when you had enemies and those from the castle who wanted to hurt you. Now you want to throw us out?'

This wasn't the first time but the villagers seemed more determined, that they weren't going to back down. But neither was John.

'We are outnumbered,' murmured Nasir.

'Aren't we always?' John said, winking, his quarterstaff horizontal.

'We can't have any bloodshed, John,' called Edward.

He was right. Anger and upset was resolvable, could eventually be patched up. But physical violence? That would leave a mark on not just the bodies of the Wickham villagers and of the outlaws: it would mar any future relationship.

'I told you John. I tried to stop them!' said Meg, appearing from out of the mob.

John, catching sight of her, didn't like her being jostled like that and so roared again at the villagers, some of whom were startled into submission.

Edward took that moment to stand before John, facing the villagers. 'That's enough!' he cried. 'That's *enough!*'

But it wasn't enough. The mob seemed possessed, intent on overpowering the outlaws until a horse galloped into the throng, stomping and breathing hard.

'What, in the name of all that is holy, is going on here?' its rider demanded to know.

Edward, John, Nasir and Much all knew that voice. It was unmistakable and sent a wave of both melancholy and happiness through them all.

The rider dismounted with elegant ease, her blue-grey habit flowing as she stood before the four men, keenly aware of the effect she was having on them and the grumbling mob behind her, that began to slowly disperse.

'Marion!' exclaimed Much. 'I mean… Sister.'

'You were right the first time,' Marion said. 'Come here and give me a hug, Much, I've missed you!'

Marion greeted Nasir next before turning to John, who had a look of thunder on his face, making her feel uncomfortable even though she understood why. Edward saw the silent exchange and stepped in.

'You've come at the right time, Lady Marion.'

They had known each other for a long time, so to him, she would always be the Lady Marion of Leaford.

'I think I did, Edward.' She gave him a sad smile. 'It's good to see you. But what exactly have I ridden into?'

'Nothing that won't blow over. In time, at least. I'll leave you be. You probably all have much to talk about.'

'Thank you,' Marion replied, her smile a little brighter now but still with an undercurrent of uncertainty. She watched Edward disperse the villagers, swallowed hard and turn to her old outlaw friends. 'Not quite the reception I was expecting. Aren't any of you going to say hello?'

'What are you doing here?' John asked.

'I'll take that as a no.'

'She's come back to join us, haven't you, Marion?' Much's cheerful disposition wasn't infectious.

'No, lad. That's not why she's here.'

Marion gritted her teeth and asked the question that had been on her lips since the moment she arrived: 'Where is he?'

'This is not a good idea,' Nasir breathed.

'Aye, you're right,' agreed John. 'It's not.'

'Robin isn't here,' Much said.

'Then where is he, Much? Will *you* tell me?'

'Come away, lad,' John said, pulling Much towards him.

'I need to see him.' Marion's persistence couldn't find purchase against John's hard stance. 'That should be his decision to turn me away, not yours.'

'Nothing good will come of this,' John said, prodding his quarterstaff into the mud around his boots.

'Nasir?'

Nasir looked away from her. He had always held great respect for Marion and all that she had given up for both Robin of Loxley then Robert of Huntingdon, but he had to agree with John's point of view. 'We do not want old wounds opening.'

'You know I wouldn't be here if it wasn't something important me,' Marion pointed out.

'Maybe that's the problem,' John replied. 'It's important to you. You could have come to see Robin at any time but now, because you need something, here you are. You broke his heart, you selfish…' John never got to finish, the slap across his face from Marion saw to that.

It was a moment that shocked them both. A visibly shaken Marion went to apologise but broke off. 'Nothing's forgotten,' was all she managed to say.

'I know where he is…'

John turned angrily. 'Meg, stay out of this.'

Meg had silently come up beside them but could stay quiet no longer. 'No, John, I won't. He's in the great barn.'

She pointed towards the main area of the village and to the largest of the outhouses.

Marion's eyes followed to where Meg's fingers were indicating. 'There?'

'Yes,' qualified Meg. 'There. You'll find him dru-.' Meg paused then sighed. 'You'll find him there.'

Marion began to walk away with John about to stop her, when Nasir held him back.

'This is between the two of them now,' the Saracen advised wisely.

John shrugged Nasir's arm away from his elbow. Meg was in his line of fire now. 'I hope you're ready to pick up the pieces. What the hell were you thinking?'

Meg didn't back down, tired of playing this long game with John. 'She's the cause of our unhappiness, John. Robin is Marion's problem. Time she faced up to what she did.'

Marion heard what Meg said but didn't look back as she neared the barn. If she was right, if they were all right, then perhaps this was the first step in getting those accusations dealt with once and for all.

'Do you think she'll be surprised at what she finds?' Much asked tentatively.

'Hard to tell,' John replied. 'We've all been through the mill these last few months. It's just that some of us have handled it differently than others, is all.'

***

The old maid was once again milking her cow.

She looked at the form asleep in the hay. If her noise woke him, it would serve him right. Sleeping the day away whilst honest folk worked. *Well, that was the nobility for you,* she thought, *if indeed he is a noble.* She didn't believe the stories herself. After all, why would anyone give up a life of privilege and comfort for this?

Robin stirred and then, perhaps in answer to her question, whispered one word in his sleep:

Marion.

As if it were a summons, the barn door was abruptly thrown open and a nun strode in and once again the old maid found herself rebuking an unwelcome visitor for the disturbance.

'Oh, I'm so very sorry, ma'am. I didn't think anyone else was in here,' said Marion, smiling at the old maid. But the nun's bright disposition was wasted.

'People never do!' came the snappy retort. 'I'm trying my best to get this old girl milked and it's bad enough him lying there all day and all night long without you lot barging in every time it eventually stops raining. What do you want?'

'To see him,' Marion said, pointing to the sprawling hay-covered man.

'For someone who does nothing, he's very popular.'

'He's Robin Hood.'

The maid peered over to him. 'No he's not,' she said seemingly with authority. 'The others called him Robin but I knows he's not.'

'Isn't he?' pressed Marion. 'Who is he, then?'

'Now,' the maid began, 'that's not what I'm entirely sure of.' Her voice lowered as if there were others hiding in the hayloft or behind bales, bringing Marion into her confidence. 'But I's sure he's not Robin Hood.'

'What if he is, though?' whispered Marion.

'Then I'll be a duck's mother because I don't believe in spirits and deaduns that walk the earth. So you mark my words. Whoever you think that is over there smelling as bad as my old girl here, you be careful.'

The maid's words cut Marion deep. The notion that Robin Hood was dead gave her a sense of unease. That Wickham's saviour and the saviour of others could no longer protect them might as easily mean that he truly was dead in their eyes.

'I'll try to remember that,' Marion said, holding back tears. What if it were true? That Robin Hood had gone and in his place was a drunken Robert of Huntingdon? 'Perhaps I am here to save this unfortunate man's soul?'

'Then you'd better be quick about it. He's making the place untidy. A fine young lady like you, married to the cloth and all, shouldn't be creeping around cowsheds in the middle of the day. But why is he so special? He don't half dream badly. Always calling out he is.'

'What kind of things is he saying? I thought perhaps I heard my name?'

'If you're Marion, then you did,' the old maid replied.

Marion looked sadly at the sleeping form. 'Will you give us few moments?'

'Eh? Oh.' The maid grumbled under her breath as she struggled up from the milking stool, her back arched, giving her a shuffling gait. 'I don't know why I lets you young 'uns tell me what to do all the time. My old mother, she'd tell me to stay where I was and not be bossed around.' She was still mumbling to herself as she left the barn, Marion shuddering as the chilly wind swept through briefly.

Now alone in the barn with Robin, Marion looked at the bucket of milk that the old woman had left. She walked over, picked it up, and then emptied its contents all over his head, causing him to sit bolt upright, spluttering and coughing. The air turned blue as he swore vengeance on whoever was responsible.

'Now there are a few choice words I haven't heard since we sat around the campfires in Sherwood.'

Robin pulled his lank, milk-sodden blonde hair from his face. He couldn't believe his eyes. It was her, standing there, as beautiful as the day she'd said goodbye to him, as beautiful as the day he first saw her in Nottingham Castle. His heart leapt, caught in his throat and he breathed out heavily.

Marion.

Then he became acutely aware of his sorry state. He stank long before she tipped the bucket of milk over him and hadn't shaved for a few weeks. He went on the attack.

'Which of them had summoned you?'

'No-one sent for me,' Marion gently protested.

But Robin wasn't in the mood for listening. 'I am fine. You've had a wasted journey. You should leave.'

Marion ignored him and came straight to the point. 'Did you know that de Rainault has been reinstated as Sheriff?'

'You came here to tell me that?' Robin spat. 'What difference does it make now? We used to live in Sherwood. It's all changed.'

'Yes, you're right, Robin. We did used to live in Sherwood. But what about now?'

'Those days are gone.'

'I'm beginning to believe they have. Look at the state of you, Robin! This isn't living, it's barely even an existence.'

'So what of the Sheriff?'

'Robin Hood and the Sheriff of Nottingham. You two will never be at peace. Just because you're hiding in a barn in Wickham doesn't mean to say he won't rekindle his obsession with you.'

'Who am I hiding from? Him?'

'In part,' she said quietly. 'But more likely from yourself.'

'I don't care. Not anymore.' Robin stood and looked her in the eye. There was still a glimmer in his own, still something that tugged at him to want to be overjoyed to see her. Perhaps he was but just couldn't admit it and perhaps, too, she was right, that he was hiding from his own feelings.

She wanted to hold him then but her bravery had left her. She could argue with barons, kings and hold her own against mercenary lords but telling Robin that she still loved him was for the moment beyond her. So instead she tried a different subject. The one she came here for.

'I don't care, either,' she lied. 'But even you have to take notice of the fact that the Sheriff himself has been robbed! His taxes. All he's collected since he retook office.'

'Serves him right,' Robin murmured.

'There was a time when such an audacious theft would have people whispering your name,' Marion replied.

'Who was it then?'

'His own men.'

'Good for them,' said Robin quietly. He daren't admit he was beginning to become intrigued by this news. 'Some things are best forgotten. That's not me anymore.'

'So you think you can just walk away from the past, forget all of it?'

'I'm trying to. But you're not exactly helping.'

'What about John and Nasir? Much looked up to you. You've turned your back on them.' Marion toed the bucket lying on its side. There was still a few drops of milk in it. 'Where's Will?'

'I don't know,' Robin sighed. He wanted Marion to stay but he was hoping she'd turnabout and leave. He didn't want this conversation. But this was his

Marion, stubborn, forthright and immovable. He was having this conversation whether he liked it or not.

'You made a promise to Herne. You're denying him now and you're wrong if you think getting drunk every day is the way to live now. And you won't like me saying this but I'm proof that the Sheriff won't forget.'

'What do you mean? You were in Halstead. You were safe. The Sheriff can't reach you in there.'

'I have come here as de Rainault's messenger, to inform you that the Sheriff wants you to recover the stolen monies and you…'

She didn't get to finish. Robin was laughing in disbelief.

***

Matthew, Edward's son, now well over half a score in age, dashed home.

'What's the matter?' Edward asked, as the boy stumbled breathlessly to a halt at the table, around which he sat with John, Nasir and Much.

Matthew was excited, his words tumbling out. Edward asked him to slow down and take a couple of lungfuls of air. 'It's… it's Robin! He spoke to me!'

When the outlaws first arrived in Wickham to make it their new home, Robin had taken Matthew fishing, spent time with him, taught him how to shoot his own bow. The hours the boy had spent in the woods just outside the village with his young friends, pretend-playing at defending the village against the evil Sheriff and his lackeys, had initially given cause for concern for his mother. And when Robin had started to withdraw into himself, finding comfort in the ale and the barn, it became clear to anyone who cared to consider it that Robin Hood was quickly becoming something other than the people's champion he had been made out to be.

Matthew had taken it personally, his young mind believing he had upset his hero somehow, and it had taken a little while for him to accept the presence of the man in the barn who rarely showed his face. The old maid who scared him and who was always in there milking her cow kept him away but he'd been waiting for the day when Robin would need his help. Matthew had faith, something Edward encouraged. No one wanted Robin to be forgotten. No one wanted him to stay that way, so when Robin had opened the barn door and, on seeing Matthew hiding by a cart, asked him to fetch the others, Matthew was overjoyed.

'What did he say, lad?' asked John.

'He wants you to go to him!'

'All of us?' queried Much.

'Yes. He asked for you, Nasir and John.'

John looked at the others, hopeful. What did he want? What had Marion said to him? There was only one way to find out.

The three outlaws dashed out and Matthew made to follow, his excitement riding high.

'No, son' Edward said calmly, a hand on his shoulder. 'Not for our ears.'

Matthew was crestfallen but listened to his father. He stopped at the doorway and watched the men go, darting across the village under clouds that were dark and brooding, turning day into night, wondering if his hero had finally returned.

***

The outlaws burst into the barn, apprehensive as to what they would find.

Robin sitting cross-legged in the hay laughing like a thing possessed.

'John..!' Robin said eventually. 'Listen… listen to this! Marion, tell them what you told me!'

'Robin,' she said, annoyed.

'No, no… Tell them!' Robin wiped his eyes with his sleeves and stood, his laughter eventually giving way to a terse glare at Marion. 'If you can make me laugh after everything, then you can make them laugh, too. *Tell. Them.*'

'Why are you being like this? You're being unfair.'

'Marion, just say it!'

'Easy on her, Robin,' John said. He had his own thoughts and reservations about Marion's return but she still deserved some respect. She had been, after all, one of them.

'It's fine, John,' Marion said, seeing that Robin was determined to have her tell the outlaws what had finally brought her here. With the embarrassment welling up within her, she told them she was here in the capacity of the Sheriff's envoy.

'What does de Rainault want?' Much asked, as surprised as any of them – and just as eager to know.

'What is it he always wants?' murmured Nasir. 'Our heads.'

'You all knew he was back,' said Robin, 'and you didn't tell me?'

'Would you have listened?' asked John. 'Would you have cared?'

Marion detailed the Sheriff's demand that Robin recover the tax monies that had been stolen. Nasir smelled a rat and said as such.

'He thought we'd do it because of you?' John asked bitterly. 'What's in it for us?'

'Do we get a pardon?' Much asked.

'Aye, lad. You can hope.'

'The Sheriff has good reason to think you'll comply, Robin,' Marion continued. 'And so do I.'

'Do you?' Robin. 'And I have to agree with John. What is in it for us?'

Marion looked at him, fighting back the tears that were threatening to overwhelm her. 'Don't do this, Robin. If you still feel anything for me, then let me explain. In private.'

Robin though was playing to the crowd and not feeling disposed to acts of charity. He ignored her pleas. 'There aren't any secrets here. Please tell everybody what is so important that you simply *have* to be the Sheriff's errand girl.'

'Damn you for this, Robin,' Marion said angrily. She hated him at that moment, hated what had happened to them. On her journey to Wickham, she'd even wondered if things would ever go back to how they were. She wasn't sure if they ever could be and she wasn't even sure she actually wanted them to be. But looking at the utter disgust on Robin's face right now told her all she needed to know. The tears stopped threatening and finally broke through. 'The reason you have to do this, the reason de Rainault thinks you will, is that if you don't, then we, you and I, Robin… we'll never see our child again. So you see, I need you to do this, too.'

A shocked silence hung over the barn.

No one quite knew what to say and the longer the silence went on, the more difficult it was to break it.

'Go,' Robin eventually said, his eyes wide and red with hurt.

John, acutely embarrassed for the both of them, knew how desperately they needed their privacy and guided Much out with Nasir following.

Robin waited until the barn door closed. It rattled on its hinges as the wind built up once more. He looked at Marion but she could hardly bear to return the gaze. 'I'm sorry.'

'A child?' Robin asked. 'Why didn't you tell me?'

'To protect you.'

'How can you even say that?' Robin replied in disbelief. 'We have a child that the Sheriff has taken. If we want to see our child again, then this is the price.' Robin walked a couple of circles and ruffled his long hair. 'Even the Sheriff knew…'

'Not by choice.' Marion assured him.

'I didn't know… but the Sheriff did! The Sheriff!' He rubbed his eyes. He hadn't slept well and was still having broken dreams. 'Why have you never told me? Do you think so little of me?'

'You must hate me.' Marion was exhausted, emotionally drained.

'I don't hate you. You know I could never do that. I'm just… just hurt.'

Marion took Robin's hand and pulled him down to the hay. They sat there and talked for hours, and the tears flowed.

***

Friar Tuck pulled back on the reigns of his horse, guiding it and the cart he sat upon into the courtyard of Halstead Abbey.

As his little caravan came to a stop two nuns, in silence, untethered the exhausted animal and led it to a trough, the water murky and green in places.

Tuck clambered down, struggling with the distance between the ground and the cart, and blew air out between his pursed lips as the Mother Superior, Abbess Constance, approached.

'I hope you have had a journey without incident, Brother Tuck,' she said.

'It went as slowly as one would expect but I am relieved to finally be here.'

'You may wish to freshen up. You can do so in the dormitories. The sisters are currently elsewhere at their chores.'

'And how is she?'

Constance paused for a moment before answering. 'Sister Marion is well. She has yet to be informed of your arrival.'

'I thank you for your benevolence in allowing me to take her confession.'

'A meal has been prepared for you.'

Tuck smiled his broad infectious smile. He hadn't eaten since before Lauds and it must have been well past Terce by now. He had felt his stomach rumbling since passing through Suffolk. 'That is most kind.'

'I have only allowed you to take Sister Marion's confession due to the nature of your mutual… past.' Constance led Tuck to the main building and a small door that led to the nuns' quarters. 'I can assure you this will not set a precedent.'

'I understand, Abbess.'

'Wash and eat as quickly as you can and you can be on your way once the confessional has been carried out.'

There's nothing like being made to feel wanted, Tuck thought to himself and did as he was bade.

***

Sometime later, with his rotund belly full and wine coursing through his veins, Tuck made himself comfortable in the tiny booth to one side of the main chapel, and waited.

What did Marion want to tell him? What was it she couldn't tell Abbess Constance? He'd heard nothing of Robin and the others in months so hoped it was not bad news about their welfare. The Sheriff had not been seen of and it was rumoured he was dead. No replacement officer had been appointed though and with Gisburne away in the land of the Muslim, Nottingham had been run by the money counters ever since.

From the other side of the modesty screen, Tuck heard someone sit down on the stool. He knew it was Marion and his nerves betrayed him as his voice quavered, 'Hello, Little Flower.'

'Hello, Tuck,' Marion replied, her own voice quiet, spirit dampened.

'Are you well? Are they looking after you?'

'Yes. Yes, the sisters and the Abbess are very kind.' A pause. 'How is Robin?'

'He no longer confides in me. Of him there is no news. As far as I know he still resides in Wickham. He is still in pain, I would imagine, but what is done is done.'

'Brother Tuck,' Marion began, formality in her address.

'Yes, Sister Marion?'

'Will you take my confession?'

'Of course.' But for the next few moments, nothing came from Marion. Tuck leaned in to the modesty screen, listening to her shallow breathing and what he sadly concluded was gentle sobbing. 'Sister?'

'I'm...'

Tuck waited again. 'Cat got your tongue?'

'I'm with child,' Marion said eventually. She repeated it, this time more sheepishly.

It was as if someone had thrown a bucket of freezing water over Tuck as he registered what she'd said. 'How?' he asked. 'Actually, never mind, I know the how,' he spluttered in a barely contained whisper. 'Are you... are you sure?'

'Yes.'

'And it is Robin's?'

'Of course it is!' replied Marion, appalled that he could even ask that!

'I'm sorry. I'm just very shocked, is all.' Now though, he had a practical question. 'Do you know by how many months?'

'It had been just after I had taken my vows.'

Tuck counted back in his head and nodded to himself, letting out a sigh. 'More to the point, why didn't you wait?'

'We were in love and Death could have reached out at any time. And it did, didn't it?' she said. 'Sometimes love and time are not kind companions.'

'Be that as it may, Sister Marion, it is incompatible with giving yourself to God.'

'I know that only too well. That's why I could never have confessed this to the Mother Superior.'

'You understand that you can no longer stay here in Halstead?'

'Yes.'

'And Robin has to be told.'

'Why?' Marion asked with indignation.

'He's the father!' exclaimed Tuck.

'That's my choice to make,' replied Marion firmly.

'I think you'll find that cannot be altered!'

'I meant it's my choice to tell him.'

'Why shouldn't he know?'

'There's no need for him to.'

'Every child has the right to know their parents. Robin would make a good father.'

'No.'

'You won't even give him the chance?'

'Protest all you like. My mind is made up.' Marion's tears had dried. She looked down at her growing belly, hidden under the folds of her habit. 'This child will not live an outlaw's life.'

'But where will you go? You intend to raise the child alone?'

'Perhaps I can place the baby with an ordinary family and watch over them from the confines of the Abbey.'

'And what of Robin?' Tuck asked.

'If he knew, he'd want us back together. He'd hate me even more than he does now,' she said. 'But there is one question I have for you.'

Tuck sighed and rested his fingers on the lip of the modesty screen. 'Yes, I will.'

On her side of the screen, Marion smiled in relief. She didn't even need to ask. Tuck was the closest thing to a family she had now and she trusted him implicitly. Having his help was, to coin an acutely apt phrase, a Godsend.

'Thank you.'

'But you should still tell Robin,'

'Are you speaking as a man?'

'What's that to do with anything? I'm not a father and never will be so the love of a child is something I will never experience,' Tuck responded. 'I am speaking as a friend.'

'*Will you tell him?*'

'*I...*' *Tuck was torn... his two friends at war with each other and now with a child involved.*

'*I don't need to remind you that this admission must stay confined to the sanctity of the confessional.*'

'*Little Flower, I know. I won't tell him. You can be assured of that. And now I have something of a confession of my own.*'

'*What's happened?*' *Marion asked, detecting regret and sadness in her old friend as he spoke.*

'*Robin banished me from Sherwood.*'

Marion gasped. '*What in God's name did you do?*'

'*Not did. Something I do and continue to do. Something very simple. Something very important to me.*'

'*What, Tuck?*'

'*I maintain a friendship with you*'

This was appalling. '*Did the others not try to intervene?*'

'*You know John. He made sure Robin knew it was wrong. But Robin... since you left, he has changed. He won't be questioned. So there won't ever be an opportunity for me to tell Robin of all this even if I was inclined to do so.*'

There was a pause. '*And what of Herne?*'

'*Herne. I asked for his audience but he wouldn't appear to me. John tried, as well.*'

'*So Robin is lost to him, too, now,*' *Marion said, sadly.*

'*There was nothing for me there. And to save whatever it was I still had, I agreed to leave.*'

'*Where did you go? And why didn't you tell me this before?*'

'*I spent time at St Teilo's church across the border before returning to England. I didn't want to be too far from you. Somehow I knew you would need me nearby.*'

'*I'm glad you're here.*' *Marion slid the modesty screen back and squeezed Tuck's hand tight.*

'*What will we do?*' *he asked.*

'*A pilgrimage?*'

'*That's a good idea.*' *Tuck smiled at her through the little portal.* '*Abbess Constance won't take the suggestion from you, though. I'll speak to her. I can't see why she won't grant us dispensation. That will be our cover. Nobody else must find out!*'

CHAPTER 5

The storm had broken again and John and the others had taken shelter in Edward's home, all waiting with apprehension as to the outcome of the meeting in the barn.

'I need some air,' John growled and opened the door. Marion was standing outside, standing in the rain. Just from her face, John knew that Robin was going to help her. She braced herself as he approached but John wasn't squaring up for a fight, quite the opposite. 'A child, Marion?' he said gently.

'I never intended you to know,' Marion replied softly.

'That is certainly clear. But the fact is we have found out. Do you really think you could have kept this a secret?'

Nasir had heard the exchange and came out to see Marion. 'This changes everything,' he said simply.

'But?' Marion asked, a hand on Nasir's broad chest.

'But we're still going to go with you and Robin,' John announced.

'We are stronger as a group, aren't we, John?' This was from Much who had followed Nasir.

Marion smiled. 'Yes. We are. We always were.'

'We have supplies to organise,' said Nasir. 'Much…'

It took a few moments but the miller's son got the hint and he excused himself, rushing after the Saracen.

It was now that Marion threw her arms around John in a warm embrace. 'Oh, John.'

'I don't like what's happened to us,' he said, returning the moment of affection.

'Me neither. But it had to be.'

'I'm sorry I didn't make you feel welcome.'

'I'm sorry I went away.'

'Is Robin alright?' John didn't want to pry but his leader's welfare had always been of importance to him.

'I think so. It may take him some time to come around to things.'

'He has missed you. He may not show it. But I can see it.'

'And I, he,' Marion said, pulling away. 'I know it's not been easy on any of you. Has Robin *really* let everything go? I'd heard he'd even turned his back on Herne.'

'It's like he became someone else.' John looked up as the rain finally desisted. It was still thunderous, however. 'Let me show you something.'

John led Marion into the hut that he shared with Meg, which (due to their avoidance of marriage vows) had been the cause of much eyebrow-raising in Wickham. He reached under their bed and located a long slim wooden box.

'What's in it?' Marion asked.

'See for yourself. Open it,' replied John.

Marion pulled back the sackcloth and gasped at what she saw revealed underneath.

There lay Albion, Robin's sword, of one the seven of Wayland the Smith, broken into pieces.

'In a fit of drunken rage, Robin had flung the blade into the trees,' John explained. 'I went looking for it and found it like this. It's damaged beyond repair.'

'But it couldn't have shattered so easily, surely?'

'That's what I thought. It's as if Herne himself took the power from it, destroyed it just as Robin destroyed any links to him.'

Marion touched the fragments. They were cold, dull, just jagged pieces of metal. The sword's inscription was dirty and obscured. The hilt was missing. She looked up at John.

'I never would have imagined Robin could have done such a thing.'

John leaned in and covered up the damaged weapon, closing the lid of the thin casket. 'Come on, Marion. Let's get going.'

***

The meeting of the outlaws took place in Edward's home.

Much looked around him: Robin, clean-shaven and sitting away from the others: John with Marion by the fire. Nasir was picking at some cooked meat as Edward made sure the door was fastened and they weren't overheard. It was like old times, even though they weren't all here. He still missed Will Scarlet and jolly old Tuck.

'The story of the Sheriff's stolen taxes is all over the shire,' Marion said, knowing that the outlaws hadn't ventured too far from Wickham the past few weeks. 'There are rumours the guilty soldiers fled north, perhaps even as far as Scotland.'

'Guilty?' Robin asked. 'Why are they guilty? They have taken what wasn't the Sheriff's. *He's* the guilty one.'

'Aye, he always is,' agreed John.

Marion knew this was a comment specifically for her. She saw in Robin's eyes that he didn't wholly trust her. 'It was a turn of phrase,' she said.

'Where were they last seen?' Robin wanted to know.

'Headed towards Barnsley,' Edward replied. 'Some of us, traders I'd sent out to buy fresh livestock, overhead some travellers talking on the Rotherham road.'

'This is our only lead. We don't have a lot of time to waste,' Robin said, determination in his voice.

Marion smiled inwardly. For the briefest of moments, the old Robin was still there.

'Then it's agreed.' John stood. 'At first light?'

'At first light,' confirmed Robin.

As everyone began to filter out into the night, Much said, 'Herne protect us.'

There was an awkward silence and Robin ducked out into the rain. John grabbed Much by the elbow and ushered him along. 'Aye, lad.'

Outside, Robin was waiting for Marion. He seemed nervous, as nervous as he was when they first spoke to each other so many years ago now.

'What do you want to ask me?' she asked.

He swallowed hard, squinting in the gloom. 'Will you… will you stay with me tonight?' he asked.

Marion couldn't meet his gaze. Suddenly she felt as embarrassed as he looked. *Yes! Of course I will, Robin! I think I wanted to but I wasn't sure.* 'I cannot,' she replied.

Robin retorted straight away. 'Or will not.'

His curt reply brought Marion's thoughts back to reality. 'You're right. I won't.'

'Why did you stay to talk to me, then?' snapped Robin, looking at the cup he had brought out with him, as if noticing it for the first time.

'You need a clear head for the morning,' she said, ignoring his question. 'I'll excuse myself', she added. And with that, Marion was gone.

Robin considered his half-empty cup. The raindrops splashed into it, mixing with the ale. After a moment, he flung the contents onto the dirty ground and stomped off towards the barn. Now he had no intention of resting. There was something he had to do before sunrise.

***

Marion and Friar Tuck arrived in Wellow before dusk.

She had visited a few times, each time to reassure herself what she intended to do. But this time it was different. This time she had her child in her arms and the sorrow of what she was about to do was overcoming her.

'Little Flower,' Tuck said, a calming presence in her upside-down life, 'are you sure?'

'You know why I don't want him to know; why he can't know. It makes us all vulnerable!' she exclaimed.

'That's not what I asked. I know why you have to do this. I want you to be sure you have to do this.'

'Yes, I'm sure.'

'I still don't believe this is the correct thing to do.'

'We don't have any other choice, Tuck.'

Marion hadn't come to this decision easily and Tuck felt uneasy in pressing the point. He wouldn't have been able to live with himself if he'd simply stood by and said nothing.

The village was quiet, pretty and on the banks of a river, streamed in some places, forded in others. The villagers had come to know Marion over the last few weeks, and greeted her warmly every time. Word had got to Geoffrey that they had arrived and so he and Esther came out to welcome them.

Marion clung tightly to her daughter. This would be the most painful goodbye she would ever had to face but Esther's smile at least gave her hope that this was the right path to take.

Seeing Marion's hesitancy and accepting now that there was no turning back, Tuck gently took the baby from her and placed her in Esther's open arms.

In a maelstrom of emotion and fighting back tears, Marion said, 'Goodbye, my sweet girl. You will live in my heart.' She kissed her daughter's forehead and turned away.

'We will look after. She will grow to be strong and proud.' Geoffrey said. But his reassurances weren't enough for Marion and she hurried away, back to the cart on the edge of the village green.

'May the Lord look over you all,' Tuck said and followed Marion.

She was already sitting at the front of the cart, staring into the distance.

'We should be going,' she said as he climbed up and sat next to her.

'I'll take you back to Halstead and from there I will return to St Teilo.'

Marion dabbed her eyes and looked at him. 'But that's in Deheubarth. Why are you going back there?'

'You have stolen Robin's right to know his child.'

Anger swelled within Marion. 'But I have saved Robin the pain of knowing! God would understand.'

'Maybe he will, but I'm not sure I do,' Tuck said gravely. 'I love you Marion. You were always my little flower and you always will be, but this… Taking this from Robin, I can't be a part of it, not anymore.'

Marion was reeling. 'But I need you!'

'No. You have Abbess Constance and the sisters.'

'But you'll visit me?'

'Not anymore. I can't.'

'But why not?'

'Because… I don't want to.'

That hit Marion like a hammerblow. 'Why are you being so cruel? This is not like you, Tuck.'

And she was right. It wasn't like him at all. But he was convinced this was the way he had to be

'I need to be away from this, from you,' he said, his voice sombre. 'To start over. I'm sorry Marion but once I've seen you safely returned to Halstead, we won't see each other anymore.'

***

Lying in her bed, Meg stared at the wattle and daub wall, the criss-cross patterns turning in on themselves as her tiredness blurred her vision. Yet she did not want to sleep and was waiting for John to come home.

She heard him bid a goodnight to Nasir outside then enter the little house, get undressed and rinse his face in the water in the bowl on the rickety table. She pretended she was asleep as he finally climbed under the rough blanket. He went to cradle her from behind but she moved slightly away. Somehow she could just sense his anticipation at the coming dawn.

'You're going to blindly follow him then?' she asked after a while…

'I thought you were asleep,' John replied. 'How did you know we were planning something?'

'You may think I'm slow—'

'I don't, lass.'

'Well, the others… they do. I'm *not* slow. I know what's going on.' She turned over to face him, her blues eyes glistening with tears. 'I was listening outside Edward's place.'

40

'You were spying on us?'

'She was there. Why couldn't I be?'

'Because…' John touched her face, relieved she didn't flinch. 'You know why. It's… different with her.'

'Because I'm not part of your group.' Now she turned her cheek away.

'Meg…'

'No. It's true.'

'I'm glad you're not,' said John, trying to turn this conversation around.

'Glad?' Meg sat up, pulling the coarse blanket up in front of her.

'Aye, lass. I wouldn't want you to be in danger if you were out there with us.'

'So you're definitely going.'

'It's late. Let's not start this again.'

'Answer me, John.'

John sighed and rolled onto his back. 'Robin needs me.'

'And what about me needing you?' Meg asked. 'What if you don't come back?'

'I *am* coming back. It's just a few days. You've got nowt to worry about.'

'So I just stay here and wait?'

'Yes…' John glanced over to her. 'Please?'

'I've waited long enough. Things need to change this time.'

'But they are different.'

'You get back out there into Sherwood, properly into Sherwood, you won't want to come back.'

'Of course I will. Don't be daft.'

'See? You *do* think I'm stupid!'

With that Meg clambered out of bed and pulled her dress on.

'That's not what I meant!'

She looked at him and shook her head. 'If you want to be with me, John Little of Hathersage, then you have a choice to make.'

'I won't be told what to do, lass!'

'But Robin tells you!

'That's…'

'Different? Yes, you keep saying that!' Meg folded her arms. 'If you go with him on this fool's errand, I won't be here if you come back.'

***

Robin had waited patiently in the tree for most of the night, listening out for the heavy footfall of strangers in the forest. He'd had time to reflect on Marion's news and wondered what would happen next. The forest was his and he knew he'd neglected it. Perhaps it was time to once more face up to his responsibilities to the poor, the dispossessed… and to Marion and his own child. Was he still their hope?

But such thoughts could cloud his judgement and he needed to stay alert. It had been a long time since he'd even stepped foot back into his beloved Sherwood and his wits needed polishing, especially in this weather.

In the moments before sunrise, he heard a horse whinnying in the distance. His instincts hadn't abandoned him completely as he silently jumped down from his safe place and padded around to behind the noise.

And there they were: three horse-mounted soldiers, two looking too old to even be out of the confines of a castle, one seemingly just weaned from his mother's breast.

Was I ever that young when carrying a sword? Robin mused.

The young soldier seemed, even by Robin watching them from cover, a volatile mix of bravado and inexperience. The old sergeant exuded many years' service and was cautious as he led them along the natural pathway.

'Remind me again why we have to be up so early?' the younger man moaned.

'It's safer,' the sergeant replied.

Not safe enough, thought Robin, as he launched an arrow, purposely missing them and impaling it on a tree just shy of the young soldier's head.

The boy pulled on his horse's reigns in shock, managing to steady the animal as the sergeant cursed himself for tempting fate.

The three horses circled, all soldiers now with swords drawn.

'We are here under the Sheriff's orders!' the sergeant called out, damning the incessant rain for obscuring his vision. 'Identify yourselves!'

The answer to his challenge froze his blood.

'Robin Hood!' the voice shouted back.

'Robin Hood?' scoffed the third rider. 'He's dead! Now show yourself! The Sheriff's business must not be delayed.'

'I assure you I'm not dead. What business is this you are on?' called Robin from his hiding place.

'None of *your* business!' the boy shouted.

'You're in my forest, so that makes it very much my business. Time to pay your taxes. Drop your swords,' Robin called out calmly.

'If you really are Robin Hood, then prove it! Show yourself!'

The two more experienced soldiers cursed their young companion for his stupidity.

'What the hell do you think you're doing? What if it is Robin Hood?' said the sergeant in a harsh whisper. 'He came back from the dead once before. I was there. I saw it!'

'No you didn't,' the boy scoffed, beginning a series of arguments between the soldiers as to who knew more about Robin Hood than the other.

'I saw him break his long-bow! Snapped it clean in two, he did! Then the Sheriff ordered us to kill him!'

'Yeah, but you didn't though, did you? Because—'

'So much the better if it is him then, because we'll kill him properly. Think of the reward!'

'Enough!' came a cry from behind them. Robin stepped into view, his face hidden by a cowl.

'The Hooded Man!' the third soldier gasped at the tall, lean figure.

'It's *a* hooded man. But is it *the* Hooded Man?' the boy observed.

'Don't be a fool!' the sergeant told him.

Robin raised his long-bow and drew it back, its arrow pointed at the trio. This could be tricky.

'There's three of us and he's only got one arrow!'

The two veterans froze in fear but the impetuous youngblood drew his sword and, before the other two could stop him, he spurred his horse on to charge. Robin's arrow smashed through the boy's chain mail, the force of the strike unseating the advancing soldier. He was dead before his body hit the ground.

Another arrow immediately appeared in the Hooded Man's long-bow and was once more aimed at the two remaining men.

'I won't ask again,' said Robin. 'Drop your swords and ride on, before I change my mind and take a poll tax.'

The two men did as they were told, their horses as panicked as they were; thundering off down the forest road.

Robin soothed the remaining animal, stepping over the lifeless body of the young soldier. Taking a life was never something he enjoyed but he had been outnumbered, albeit by his choice, and the impetuous youth could quite have easily maimed him.

***

John woke up with a start as dawn was breaking over the village.

He looked over to Meg but her place in their bed by his side was empty. He patted the slight indent where she had been but it was cold. She hadn't been there for a little while.

Getting dressed, he dashed out to begin frantically searching for her. None of the village's early risers had seen her. Nasir and Much had been woken by the crow of the cockerel, and were bringing their horses out of the barn when John spotted them. They hadn't seen Meg either. It was the same story when Edward arrived with Marion. She had changed out of her habit and was wearing an outfit not unlike that which she used to wear when she was part of the outlaw gang: a long, pale green tunic with breeches and boots and a quiver over her shoulder and long-bow in her grip. There was a small knife in a sheath on her hip.

Marion noted the pain on John's face. 'You don't have to do this,' she said. 'It's not your fight.'

Her gentle tones eased John's anxiety. 'But I can't abandon you,' he still replied.

'You wouldn't be. Robin will understand.' Marion reassured him.

However, Robin's own absence from this early morning gathering had not gone unnoticed. If he'd drunk himself to sleep again, they needed to find him quickly and sober him up.

'We should start looking for Robin now,' said Nasir. 'The day will not wait.'

'It doesn't need to,' announced Robin, as he walked towards them, carrying his bow with a horse by his side.

'Been hunting?' Much asked.

'I needed a new blade,' Robin responded, his newly acquired sword hanging from his waist. 'Are we ready?'

'We were just…' John began.

'Meg's gone,' Marion explained. 'We were all about to help John look for her.'

'You don't need to,' John replied, and began to call out Meg's name.

Robin looked at his friend. 'You should stay and get things sorted,' he said.

John shook his head. He had resigned himself to the inevitable. 'She's made her choice and so have I,' he said. 'Which is my horse?'

Robin smiled. It felt good to be among his friends again, ready to ride out. Their adventures came with danger but he knew that there was always a purpose to everything they did.

This time, the purpose was more personal than anything ever before.

Nasir led a large mare to John, her shaggy mane the same shade as John's own. 'For you.'

John laughed, noticing the similarity. Nasir wasn't known for his sense of humour but it was there for his friends when he deigned to show it.

The group mounted up.

'North, then!' ordered Robin, as they turned their horses and began to make their way out of Wickham.

Edward watched them recede into the distance as the thunderclouds returned overhead. Matthew stood by his side, excited to see his heroes together again after all this time.

'Good luck to you, Robin,' Edward said quietly. 'May Herne protect you. May Herne protect you all.'

CHAPTER 6

Three days had gone by since the band had left Wickham. The sun was beginning to set and everyone was tired and hungry.

They had made good progress on their journey, and as they began to make camp in a small clearing deep within the forest just outside Worsborough, Robin approached Marion.

'I'm sorry you've had to live rough these past few days. It has to be a world away from the comfort and safety of Halstead.'

Marion sighed. 'I'm not a fragile clay pot that needs wrapping up in linen, Robin,' she snapped. 'I was living "rough" in Sherwood long before you.'

Robin didn't need reminding of that. In fact, Marion's existence in Sherwood before he took on the mantle of the Hooded Man had been part of his uncertainties which had led him to start finding answers in the bottom of a beer barrel. Even though Herne had crowned him the King of Sherwood, for many years he felt he'd lived in another man's shadow. But he'd eventually come to accept and understand Herne's decision and was fully aware that maybe one day another Robin Hood would carry the honour once his own life was over.

But to still be jealous of a dead man was ridiculous. Marion had loved him and they had had a child together.

'In the first few weeks after you left,' Robin explained, 'I thought you would realise your mistake and come back. But, no. When the weeks turned to months then into a year and more, I had to stomach the bitter realisation that all hope was lost.'

'Please don't do this,' Marion begged. 'I had my reasons.'

'I was just so… so angry.'

'I understand that.'

They stared in silence at the fire Nasir had built.

'We've spent all this time talking about our child, Marion, but I have no idea whether we have a boy or a girl.'

A smile played across Marion's lips. 'I was wondering when you'd ask. Robyn is a gift from heaven.'

The outlaw's heart leapt in his chest. 'Robin! What is he like? Is he like you?'

Marion began laughing. 'Robyn is a girl! We have a daughter. A beautiful little girl!'

'A girl! If she's beautiful, then she is like you!' Robin wanted to grab Marion then, pull her close and never let her go. 'I can't be angry with you anymore,' he said suddenly.

Then, Marion found herself trying to explain it all. 'I… When I thought you were dead. I couldn't take that pain, not again. Can you understand that?'

Back to him again. The other Robin. She couldn't take that pain again.

Marion saw the look on his face. 'I loved you. I never thought I would. I never thought I could. But I did. So very, very much. And seeing you dead…'

'I can understand it, but it wasn't me that was dead. It was one of Gulnar's vile creations.'

'I know that, but still…' Marion said gently.

'It felt like you were blaming me for your own fears,' Robin said.

'Perhaps I was. But my feelings haven't changed.'

Robin shifted to face her, the sheepskin he was sitting on becoming damp from the incessant rain. 'Haven't they?'

Marion avoided his gaze. 'I needed to put it all behind me; to close it off,' she said. 'It was the hardest thing I've ever had to do.'

'More difficult than giving away our daughter?' asked Robin.

'I had to,' Marion replied, the strength in her fading.

'Marion… I'm not looking to battle against you with this. I said it because I want to understand the choice you made, what you had to face.'

'It all became too much.'

Robin nodded and held her hands. She didn't flinch, didn't pull them away. Robin needed to understand too that there was no blame anymore. She didn't want to fight, either.

'Where is our daughter?' Robin asked.

'In Wellow,' replied Marion. 'She's with the head man there.'

Robin frowned. Wellow. That was some distance from Sherwood but he recalled they had all gone there some time ago when rescuing one of his father's men from local outlaws. He hadn't realised the place had had such a lasting effect on her.

'Geoffrey?' Robin queried.

'Yes, and his wife Esther. They already have a child, a boy named after his father.' Marion explained. 'They let me visit from time to time.'

'What made you choose them?'

'They were so kind to me when we'd been released from the mercenaries. Your father's friend was in such a terrible state. He was injured. Remember we didn't think he'd survive?'

'Yes, I remember. Fairbanks was a good man. It was a shame what happened to him in the end.'

'Well, Geoffrey and Esther, they literally nursed him back to health. And when it came to the decision as to who we could trust with Robyn...'

'We?' Robin noted, 'so you had help then?'

Marion looked across at him. It wasn't very noble to pretend that he didn't know she was talking about Tuck. Robin now looked embarrassed and hesitantly asked how the Friar was.

'He's well. We've tried so very hard to keep it all a closely-guarded secret.'

'Not close enough, obviously.' Robin scoffed.

'I really don't know who told the Abbot and the Sheriff,' sighed Marion, 'But, well, here we are.'

They were interrupted by Nasir walking with stealth towards them, a finger at his lips, beckoning them to be silent.

'What's the matter?' Robin whispered.

'I feel... uneasy,' Nasir replied. 'We are being watched, I am sure of it.'

Robin bade Marion stay where she was and moved off with the Saracen to the edge of their camp. The two men scanned the trees on either side of the forest track. As they strained their senses, there was nothing. All was as it should be.

'Perhaps I am seeing shadows where there is only sunlight,' Nasir said, finally relaxing a little. 'Let us go back to the others.'

'I trust your instincts, Nasir. I think we should be wary.'

As they returned to the centre, Nasir tensed. With the light fading fast, the outlaws scanned the trees. But there was nothing. Robin brought the group together and they exchanged glances, listening to Nasir's concerns. But nothing more gave rise to Nasir's worry so, with a sigh, he too let his swords drop and shook his head. Was he getting too old?

As they relaxed, they began to talk again, Much excitedly telling stories of his and John's exploits after Marion's departure. Robin had put his blade down by his feet. Nasir was preparing some rabbits, vegetables bubbling in a pot.

Then the men came screaming out of the shadows from all sides, chaos erupting.

Whoever they were, they knew the outlaws.

They went for Nasir first, the most efficient and skilled, and cornered him by a tight gathering of trees. Both swords drawn, he cut and parried, lunged and swung, yet the five men were larger, heavier, armour giving them the advantage. But Nasir was nimble and launched himself up a tree and over their heads. He wasn't about to give up just yet.

Robin took on two of the assailants, a well-placed thrust of his new sword, felling one of them, allowing him to kick out at the other. But just like Nasir's, they were big, heavy men. Robin was struck about the neck and fell in a daze to the wet forest floor, seeing Much struggling under another of the brutes before he was clouted across the face by a metal gauntlet.

John roared in anger, pushing a line of the men to the ground in a flurry of limbs and weapons. Nasir jumped down from above and the two outlaws stood back to back, spinning slowly, taking in the full view of the forest around them.

Marion was gagged and bound, struggling as best she could, while Robin, unconscious, was roped to a tree with Much.

'They have come prepared,' Nasir said.

'Do you recognise them?' John hissed.

'No. But their fighting style is heavy-handed. They would be more at home in the bear pits.'

The strangers, the ones who hadn't been killed or knocked out by Robin's men, regrouped and surrounded John and Nasir, closing in on them.

The result was never in doubt.

Down John went, growling 'til the very last. Nasir's anger at being overcome did nothing for him either, even though he valiantly struggled while he too was tied to a tree.

As Robin regained consciousness, blurred vision slowly clearing, one of the strangers walked up to him, nose to nose.

'What are you doing in my forest?'

'Your forest?' Robin asked. It was then he noticed that Marion wasn't bound to a tree but standing, arms tied, next to one of the attackers.

The man gave him a pitying look. 'All this is Barnsley. My territory. I am Mouchard. Know the name well,' Mouchard scoffed. 'You have exceeded your own lands, I feel. Men!' He ordered them to mount up, securing the outlaws' horses to their own. 'Bring the woman!'

Marion tried to resist but was ungainly lifted onto the back of a stout-looking steed. Robin began to twist and strain against his bonds.

'Marion!'

'What use is a nun to you? She's very pretty, at least,' Mouchard leered. He moved to the fire, stamped it out, tipped the stew out over the ground and hung the rabbits from his horse's saddle.

'Touch her and I swear you will die,' Robin said, menace lacing his tone.

'She's clearly more your type, then. No, my friend, I will not touch her as she is worth a good ransom. If you can free yourselves, come find me. Perhaps we will do business, no?' Mouchard leapt onto his horse and led his men by torchlight, with Marion their prize, out of the clearing, and disappeared into the dark.

'John…' Robin began. 'Can you get free?'

'Aye, Robin. I think so. They may hit hard but they need teaching a lesson or two with rope craft.'

'They knew us,' Nasir said.

'How can you be sure?' Robin replied.

'They asked you what use a nun is to you,' he explained.

'And? We know Marion is a nun, now. What's your point?' John wanted to know.

'But how do *they* know?' asked Nasir.

Robin had caught on to what Nasir was getting at. 'She's not dressed as one!'

'Then we were ambushed!' John exclaimed but his rising anger was dampened by Much's sudden tearful cry. 'What's the matter, lad? They come back?'

'N-no…' Much stammered, having never quite completely lost his fear of the dark. 'I saw something.'

'It's your imagination. Concentrate on getting loose,' Robin said, calmly.

'There's something out there! Something flashed in the darkness!'

'What, lad?'

'Eyes!' Much cried out in terror. 'Eyes looking at me! The eyes of devils!'

'There's no such thing,' John said, trying to reassure their younger companion.

Then they heard the howling. The unmistakable spine-chilling cry of a wolf.

'Did you hear that? There *are* devils!' Much began to panic but the more he struggled, the more he got tangled up in his bonds.

'John, hurry!' cried Robin. 'I can't get free!'

The single howl had turned into a chorus, one that seemed to be constantly swelling in number and coming from every direction. The wolves were becoming bolder and eager to move in for the kill, the outlaws began to lash out with their feet whenever one of the pack got too adventurous. They were also screaming and shouting in an effort to frighten the animals away, but that strategy could only last so long.

Slavering jaws snapped at them and Much was pinning himself tightly against his tree. Robin caught one of the beasts square in the face. It yelped and jumped back, wary, but ready to pounce with a vengeance.

Just when it seemed that the wolves were gaining the final advantage, a fiery arrow came flying into the clearing. It landed with an eruption of flame that sent the wolves scattering.

'They're a poor shot, whoever they are!' John cried as claws caught his shins.

'The arrow. It was not aimed at us,' Nasir called back.

The creatures re-grouped and quickly returned. But, a second, third and fourth fiery arrow thudded into the ground and erupting an explosion of flame. The wolves were thrown into howls of panic, driven back into the forest once and for all.

As a strange calm began to settle over the clearing, the outlaws saw the light of a torch working its way towards them through the trees. Was it friend or foe?

Regardless, the approaching figure was making no secret of their presence, stumbling through the forest, huffing and wheezing.

John began to laugh. He recognised those sounds.

'John?' Robin queried.

All was revealed as the newcomer waddled into the clearing. Framed in the firelight was a rotund figure with a longbow over his shoulder and, in a familiar voice, said:

'Hello, little flowers!'

'Tuck!' exclaimed the group in unison.

'Are we seeing things?' John asked, as the flickering torchlight plunged Tuck in and out of the shadows that danced around him.

'He is a welcome sight indeed,' said Nasir.

'What are you doing here?' Much wanted to know, relieved that such a face had replaced the devils around them.

'Barnsley is home now,' the Friar said.

'You didn't go *too* far then,' John replied.

'Far enough – but good job for you I didn't go further,' Tuck said. 'I heard the pack and knew something was up. Your shouting carried on the wind, and lucky it did!'

'Well, stop the small talk and come untie us!'

With that, Tuck impaled the torch into the wet ground and took his blade to the ropes holding them captive. One by one, John, Much and Nasir embraced him and exchanged warm greetings. At last, Tuck came to Robin. With little more than a glance at each other, the blade was swung and the final set of bonds cut and immediately, Robin launched himself forward, knocking Tuck to the ground.

The friar was unable to fend off Robin's attack but John was quick enough to haul the blonde man away, Robin landing heavily on his side.

'No more fighting amongst ourselves!' John roared.

Robin had caught his lip and dabbed at the welling blood. 'You should have told me, Tuck!' Robin growled. 'You should have told me about my daughter! How long did you know?'

Much and Nasir helped Tuck to his feet, the friar visibly shaken. But he understood Robin's anger. 'What she told me was under the sanctity of confession. I took vows of silence in that regard,' he answered calmly.

'To hell with your vows!'

'Which is exactly where I would be, if I had broken them!' Tuck shouted back, 'Besides, it was for Marion to tell you. Not me.'

The two men stood staring at each other, breathing heavily.

'If Will were here, I know what he'd say,' John said.

Robin glared at John then turned away from Tuck. What was happening to them, Robin wondered. Was it a mistake to have come on this journey? To have brought most of them back together? Too much had gone by that not everyone, including Robin (which he himself acknowledged), was yet able to overcome. Even Herne had remained silent to him, something he wasn't entirely surprised about.

In the dark, the wolf pack howled again.

'I live not far. I suggest we find safe haven,' Tuck said.

'All of us?' Robin asked.

Tuck didn't look at him, instead picking up the burning torch and moving off through the trees. Without turning back, he replied, 'Until first light, at least.'

***

No one spoke as they walked towards Tuck's hut until they were all safely inside, with a roaring fire warming their feet and a hearty stew filling their stomachs.

'...and so, here we are,' Robin was saying.

Tuck looked deep into the fire, reflecting on Robin's explanation of why they were in Barnsley.

'It's not an enviable position to be in, especially now that Marion has been taken.'

'Do you think there is a connection?' asked John.

'Between the mercenaries and the Sheriff's blackmailing scheme?' Tuck shook his head. 'I don't know, but I'm willing to lay money on the mercenaries coming down from Barnsley itself.'

'Why are you so sure?'

'A few weeks ago, John, the town was overrun. Heavily-armed men took over, took hostages. Pillaged many of the storehouses. Burned a lot of the homes.'

'Didn't anyone do anything?' asked John.

'Not against battle-hardened mercenaries,' Tuck replied.

'And so they get away with it,' said John bitterly.

'Seems so, yes,' said Tuck, sighing heavily. 'Since then, the town has become a heaven for any, and all criminals.'

'Like us?' questioned Much.

'We may be outlaws but we're not criminals,' Robin said gently.

'Even if de Rainault disagrees.' Nasir reminded them.

'He's the biggest crook of them all,' said John.

'But this isn't right,' added Nasir.

'Always suspicious, eh, Nasir?' John teased.

'No.' Nasir looked at him hard, then at each of them in turn. 'John, Much… Remember the merchant…'

'Jonas?' Much said.

'Yes,' Nasir nodded. 'One merchant, accompanied by armed guards just for coins made of wood. Then we are told the Sheriff's men who stole his taxes are seen in Barnsley. Then Tuck tells us of these mercenaries raiding Barnsley… the same ones who knew where we were and took Marion. And they knew she was a nun.'

'We are better than this, to be ambushed in a forest. Somebody is a step ahead of us,' John said.

'Who?' Much asked. 'The Sheriff?'

Robin sat back against the wall of Tuck's hut. 'No. He keeps his business close to Nottingham, It's this Mouchard. He seems like an opportunist. He sees Marion as capital, something to bargain with.'

'Bargain with who, though, Robin?'

'I don't know, Much. We'll have to wait until the morning before we can go anywhere. It's not safe with the wolves on the prowl. Besides, if ransom is what the mercenaries want, Marion won't be harmed.'

'For the time being at least,' finished Tuck.

Robin voiced a sudden thought. 'If criminals are paying for the privilege of protection in Barnsley, then isn't it possible our tax thieves have sought safety behind the town's walls as well?'

'Maybe not a coincidence, then. Two birds?' Nasir asked, letting the question hang in the air.

Robin now looked at Tuck. Would he help them? Would he help him?

'For the sake of Marion, yes, I will. But after all is done, you can leave me in peace and go back to Sherwood.'

'What of forgiveness?' Nasir asked.

'I grant you forgiveness,' Tuck replied, 'and understanding.'

'And friendship?'

The question had come from Robin.

'I think we both know that faded a while back,' Tuck said sadly. 'Now, if there are no objections, I am going to get some sleep before it gets light.'

CHAPTER 7

Barnsley was a relatively large town, its sum total of two hundred residents living in constant fear of Mouchard and his men, after them having staked a claim there.

The interlopers had watched the villagers desperately fighting the fires they had purposely started, drinking heavily and harrassing all who came along to help. A few brave locals stood up to them, only to be beaten to unconsciousness or pushed into the roaring flames, laughter and abuse all the way.

Having been paraded through the village by Mouchard, Marion was exhausted and struggled to put one foot in front of the other. She slumped to the ground outside a dingy alehouse but Mouchard pulled her to her feet.

'No time to sleep yet, my beauty,' he leered into her face. 'You are the guest of honour.'

Marion was pushed into the building, the stink of male sweat, beer and blood hitting her nostrils. A great cheer rose up at her appearance, as if these inebriated men hadn't seen a woman in years.

A man stepped forward, taller and more muscular than any of the mercenaries she'd encountered before. With his shaved head and heavy beard growth that couldn't disguise the scar on his left cheek, he was a man clearly used to getting what he wanted. Marion stared at him defiantly, standing as straight as she could, the bindings on her wrists cutting into her skin. Mouchard knelt before this giant, head bowed.

'Patron,' he said.

'Do you men have no God?' Marion asked.

'She has spirit, this one. Just as we were led to believe, eh, boys?' the giant roared, thumping Mouchard on both his shoulders with palms the size of hams. 'You have done well. Be standing.'

'And who exactly are you?' said Marion.

'I am Bertrand.'

'And is this…' Marion looked around, 'your alehouse?'

'It is unwise to ridicule our leader,' Mouchard hissed, on his feet and his face in Marion's.

'It is fine, Mouchard.'

'She is a nun, patron,' Mouchard replied. 'She should know better.'

'Then she has holy spirit, eh!' Bertrand exclaimed, as the two men laughed.

Marion sighed and rolled her eyes. 'I demand you release me.'

'And where would you go, Sister?'

'Back to my friends.'

She was about to continue when Bertrand held up his hand and looked seriously at Mouchard. 'Are they alive?' he asked.

'They are. We waited to make sure,' Mouchard replied. Bertrand nodded and turned his gaze back to Marion.

'We were on a mission for my Lord Robert de Rainault, the High Sheriff of Nottingham.' She could feel the bitter taste of his full name in her mouth, but she hoped it would sound imposing to these arrogant men. 'Impeding it has serious consequences.'

Bertrand smiled. 'Next you will be telling me that the snivelling idiot Sir Guy of Gisburne will himself come to your rescue!'

'You know the Sheriff's equerry?' Marion asked. Who *were* these mercenaries?

'I am aware he is elsewhere at the moment. But your mission continues, even now. Soon, you will see that. However, for the present you shall remain our… guest before returning to Halstead.'

At this Marion was shocked. 'How do you know where I'm from?' she asked.

'Knowledge is our business,' Bertrand replied with a smile. He then pointed at one of the men standing in the gloom. 'Undo her bonds. Take her to her chambers. She needs to be in one piece.' As a guard eagerly stepped forward and untied her before leading her out of the alehouse, Bertand turned to Mouchard. 'I think you were a little rough with her. We are under instructions that no harm is to come to her. See to it she is not touched again.'

***

Marion was led to the gaol house wherein, along a couple of short stone corridors, she was brought to a halt before two sturdy, locked cell doors. During that time the guard had said nothing, his face obscured by a helmet.

'What will my fate be?' she asked him, not really expecting any sort of reply.

The guard, a set of keys appearing in his gloved hands, paused before opening one of the doors. His helmet swung towards Marion and, at her surprise, he removed it slowly. When she saw the face beneath, she nearly cried with relief.

'Will!'

'What the hell are you doing here?' he growled, in a low voice. 'As soon as I saw them bring you before Bertrand I stayed close by.'

Marion didn't answer but, instead, asked the same question of him.

Will Scarlet sighed. 'It's complicated.'

'What happened?' asked Marion, 'What is so complicated? Oh, it is good to see you. These past few days have been giddying. Did Robin send you?'

With that, Will unlocked the door and bundled Marion into the tiny cell, following her and making sure they hadn't been followed. He pulled the door so it was nearly closed.

'No, he didn't send me. I want nothing to do with that man anymore.'

'Then why the secrecy?'

'There ain't no secrecy.'

'We're in a tiny prison and you're whispering. Why not reveal who you were earlier?'

'Because of how you'd react.'

'Does Mouchard and Bertrand know you were once part of Robin's men?'

Will didn't answer. Marion pressed him again but he was uncomfortable. 'Look, this is my life now. I've accepted it. Why doesn't anybody else? It's my life!'

'I understand. I've had to make some awful decisions since going to Halstead.'

'Are you still part of the nunnery?'

'Yes. That won't change.'

'Your clothes tell me otherwise.'

'A wimple and a habit aren't exactly inconspicuous in Sherwood.'

'Guess not.'

Marion sat on the pile of hay in the corner of the cell. 'Will, tell me what happened between you and Robin.'

'Why? It's not important.'

'It's important to me. All of us, we're estranged now. Robin and me. Tuck and me. Tuck and everybody. You're here on your own.'

'How's knowing going to help?'

'It's… it's not. I just need to know.'

Will looked down at his booted feet, and breathed out hard. 'It was sometime after you left,' he began. 'We'd raided a convoy and it was a nasty fight. All but one of the men at arms was dead, and the one that was left was in bad shape. Robin was going to finish him but John held him back. The job was done and murdering in cold blood wasn't us – at least as far as John was concerned.'

'And you didn't agree.'

'It was men like that who had driven you away from Robin. Why should they have lived? I said this to Robin who warned me, warned *me*, to stay out of it, that you leaving was nobody's business but yours and his. I said to Robin that he should direct his anger like I do to scum like that. If we get rid of them, then I said to him maybe you'd come back.'

'Did you believe I would have done?'

'I don't know. I don't know if he did either but he went for me. He actually went for me! John got involved like he usually did, pulled us apart. If he hadn't, well…'

'You wouldn't have gone that far to have killed Robin, Will. I know you. You wouldn't do that to one of your own.'

'Maybe I would, maybe I wouldn't. But in any case John said we should get the convoy's money bags and get it sent around to the needy. Tuck sorted out the soldier's wounds and we stuck him back on the empty cart to Nottingham. The Sheriff's brother was there and in charge, I think. I dunno. But Robin… he didn't care about the money anymore.'

'Robin isn't the same.'

'Yeah, he ain't. He just walked away. That's when he went to Wickham for good. He was already drinking heavy before then anyway. John told me he was hurting, hurting over you. Tuck went on about keeping wounds open or some rubbish he usually spouted.'

'And you let Robin go off?'

'Well, I wasn't going to wrap him up in silks. Nah, not me.' Will looked at the helmet in his hands, its crude finish and sharp edges. 'But it was what John said that really wound me up.'

'What?'

'He said I've never gotten over the death of my wife. I could've killed 'im for saying that. He said he thought I wanted Robin to feel the same way.'

'But being in constant pain… that's no way to live.'

'Yeah, that's what Nas said.' Will looked at Marion as she stood. 'So I left. I was done. Looking after myself from now on – that was what I was going to do. I asked if anyone wanted to join me but no one answered. Their silence told me everything.'

'But you blame Robin for walking away yet you did the same thing.'

'Nah. It was different with me. John said that they all felt the same. Tuck said they were going to help Robin through it. But it's not the same. They don't know how it feels. So yeah, perhaps I did want Robin to be in pain. I told John he could go to hell. All of them could.'

'Did John try to stop you from leaving?'

'He said I was on my own if I kept going. It would be for good. And yeah, I kept going. I don't need them.'

The cell door opened just then, and one of the other mercenaries, a lieutenant to Bertrand, entered.

'What are you doing in here?' he spat. 'The prisoners are to be kept in the same cell.'

Will glared at the man and raised his eyebrows to Marion, indicating that she went along with what was about to happen next.

'Get out, you!' Will roared to Marion. 'Don't cross me again.'

He pretended to raise a fist to her and Marion feigned being terrified of him.

'Don't hit her!' the mercenary said. 'We have our orders she's not to be harmed, remember? Take her into the other cell.'

As Will led Marion back out into the narrow corridor, the mercenary stomped off. Will pulled her in close. 'I get the feeling you're hiding something.' He unlocked the second of the two cells. 'What's your secret, Marion? What don't I know?'

'It seems like the whole world knows, so you might as well, too.' Marion swallowed hard. 'Robin and I… we have a daughter.'

'A daughter!' exclaimed Scarlet, before pushing the cell door open. As he did so, what Marion saw inside left her in no doubt that this was where she needed to be.

'Robyn! Esther!' she cried, running in to embrace them.

'You know them?' asked Scarlet.

'Yes I know them. This is my daughter, Will. I hid her with Esther so that Robyn could live in peace.'

'You called her Robyn,' Scarlet said softly.

'I suppose that tells its own story,' Marion replied, her eyes fixed on little Robyn. 'What are you doing here?'

Esther looked up at Marion, fear and confusion in her expression. 'They took us from our home.'

'The mercenaries?'

Esther nodded. 'They only wanted the two of us.'

'But… why? We were set a task by Nottingham's sheriff which is meant to secure your safety.'

'I don't know any sheriff in Nottingham. Our own one, Russel de Corbeau… he doesn't have much to do with us.'

'Lucky you,' Marion breathed. 'Nottingham's can't keep his nose out of anyone's business. What did your captors say to you? Did they threaten you?'

'Marion,' interrupted Will. 'I need to get back. Mouchard will grow suspicious.'

'Of course.' Marion smiled at him as he went to leave. 'And thank you.'

'For what?'

'For being kind, Will. Even though I accept your allegiances have changed now, it's… comforting to know you're nearby.'

Will nodded once and left and Marion heard the lock clunk with a jangle of iron keys. She turned back to Robyn, leaning in to take her daughter from Esther.

Esther shrunk back, moving an arm over Robyn's frame. 'No.'

Marion was surprised and somewhat hurt. 'I just want to hold her. I'm not going to take her back.'

'It doesn't feel right. She thinks I'm her mother now. You holding her would just confuse things.'

'It's only for a few moments. Please?'

But Esther wouldn't even let Marion stroke Robyn's fiery hair. 'You made your choice.'

'But Esther… it was for her own good!'

'Yes, and I'm protecting her now! Me. Her *mother*.'

Marion sank to the floor on the other side of the cell, holding back tears. Why couldn't Esther see she meant no harm?

***

The sun was beginning to set and, from their position within the foliage, Much and Nasir were looking at the town gates of Barnsley.

From within, sounds of raucous behaviour carried on the wind. The town was a lively, well-lit, and well-guarded place.

The two outlaws were about to make their way back to camp when Much grabbed Nasir's arm and pointed with a gasp. They both now looked at the man who had just come into view and was staring out of the gate.

60

'So *that* is what happened to him,' Nasir whispered sadly.

'Should we tell him we're here? He might help us.'

'That is not a good idea.'

Much sighed, begrudgingly accepting Nasir's logic, and so they watched Will Scarlet scan the trees in their general direction, straining to see in the dusk. Then they saw the guard on duty walked over and say something to Will, who in response shook his head, turned on his heel and walked back into town.

In the trees, Much stood to take a closer look. Nasir shoved him back down.

'Keep out of sight.'

'But Nas, what if he's seen us? He might be wondering what we're doing here.'

'That question is not what you should be asking,' Nasir responded, confusing young Much. 'I do think we may have been detected. But is Scarlet friend or foe?'

Much was about to answer in indignation when Robin and John came up to them.

'The other side of the town has a guard, too,' Robin said. 'I might take some flighty feet to get past them.'

'We saw Will!' Much revealed.

Robin pursed his lips. 'Are you sure? Nas?'

Nasir nodded, which was all the confirmation he needed.

'That changes things,' growled John.

'It does?'

'Of course it does, Robin!'

Robin looked at them in turn. 'We still go in at dawn.'

'And what about Will?' John asked.

The question hung in the air and remained unanswered even as Robin, John, Tuck, Nasir and Much crept through the town gate with ease in the early morning haze. If Barnsley had been well-guarded last night, it certainly wasn't now. Inside, they saw the reason why. The sentries were out cold.

'You've all lost your touch,' Will scolded as he suddenly appeared behind them. 'I 'eard ya coming. It was lucky I knocked these lot out. They would've 'eard ya, too.'

'I never thought I'd see you again Scarlet,' John said, keeping his voice low.

'Small world isn't it,' he replied. 'I suppose you're here for Marion?'

Robin nodded, wary of Will and his temperamental nature.

Nasir held Much back. 'Careful,' he said. Much nodded.

'This way then,' whispered Scarlet. The outlaws hesitated. 'Well come on!'

As they walked nervously through the deserted streets, Robin knew that something wasn't quite right.

'How far's the gaol, Will?' he asked.

'Just through the square here,' was Scarlet's reply as they walked into the centre of the town.

There was no one around. The market stalls were absent. None of the traders who usually slept under them during market week were present, either. The whole place was strangely quiet.

'Where has everybody gone?'

Robin got his answer as the portcullis clanged to a thunderous close behind them. Everyone spun around save for Will, who simply unsheathed his sword.

Then, from out of the grain stores, stables, outhouses, the mercenaries appeared, some on the narrow battlements, some on the low straw roofs, but all armed with crossbows and all pointed at Robin and his men. Will stepped back, his distancing himself from them undeniable.

Bertrand appeared from behind his men.

'Welcome, Robin Hood. I applaud you and your men on an audacious entry into our fair town.'

'You know who we are?' Robin asked as he was relieved of his weapons.

'I know you must have many questions,' Bertrand said. 'I will be happy to answer them in time.'

Now without his quarterstaff, John clenched his fists and began to grind his teeth. There was murder in his eyes as he stared at Will. 'You betrayed us, you bas—'

A crossbow bolt landed at John's feet and he looked around at the mercenaries, searching for the one who dared fire it. He wasn't scared of them. Right now, he wasn't scared of anything.

'John…' warned Robin, knowing what his old friend was thinking. He was thinking it too but knew they all had to stay calm – but still John lunged at Scarlet, only to be held firmly by several of the mercenaries who quickly moved to intercept him.

Scarlet walked up to the giant, who was still dwarfed by the mercenaries. 'The last time we were together John, you accused me of wanting Robin to be in constant pain. Well I'll settle for you, for a few minutes at least,' he said, and then launched a terrific punch into John's stomach.

As John doubled over in pain, Robin tried to move towards Scarlet but he too was now held firmly by the men surrounding them.

Breathing hard and on his knees, John looked up at Scarlet with hatred in his eyes. 'If the last thing I ever do, Will Scatlock, is to put you in your grave, then I will die a happy man.'

'Don't use that name,' hissed Will. 'It's not yours to say. I'm Scarlet!'

'Enough!' Bertrand called out. 'This reunion is tedious. My name is Bertrand. I think you have already met my man Mouchard and, of course, Scarlet you know,' he said cordially. 'What brings you all to Barnsley?'

'We are not here to cause you harm,' said Robin. 'There's no bad blood between us, Bertrand. I see no reason why you shouldn't set us free and let us leave with Sister Marion.'

'But your reason for being here is..?' asked Bertrand again.

'We're looking for a group of fugitives from Nottingham to bring them to justice,' explained Robin. 'Hand them over and you will be well compensated.'

Bertrand considered the offer, a smile creeping over his lips. 'You're the only fugitives from Nottingham that I know of,' he exclaimed, pointing at Robin and his men.

'They proclaim to be the Sheriff's men,' said Robin. 'We have word that they were seen on the road to here.'

'Seen by whom?' Bertrand asked.

Robin looked at Bertrand and his men. Nasir, at his side, leaned in. 'I grow suspicious of his questions. He plays with you. He already knows the answers you will give.

'Your Saracen dog is right,' Bertrand said, John's anger swelling at the insult directed towards his friend. 'It is all part of us knowing how to preserve the rule of law. Don't you agree, my Lord?'

Bertand stepped aside to allow a small figure to walk into view.

'Indeed, Bertrand, and you have my thanks for delivering these criminals to me,' said Robert de Rainault.

CHAPTER *8*

'Hello, Huntingdon,' the Sheriff said with venomous glee.

'What the hell is going on?' asked John.

'Isn't it obvious? Your capture at last, you vile outlaws.'

'Then, the men we've been looking for, the theft of those taxes..?' Robin trailed off, everything suddenly falling into place in his mind.

De Rainault smiled. 'Only now do you see. This is all a fiction. And a convincing one, at that.'

'You went to great expense to plant this across the shire,' Robin said, wondering if the odds were truly stacked against them this time.

John still wasn't quite sure of what he was hearing, but Tuck was.

'We've been chasing phantoms, John. Chasing them straight into a very clever trap. Even the kidnapping of Marion by Mouchard was designed to keep us on the right path, pushing us to where De Rainault needed us all to be.'

'As astute as always, Friar Tuck,' the Sheriff purred as Jonas appeared from out of one of the stables. 'Meet my new steward – although I think a couple of you may have already met him. He takes great delight in being my gamekeeper.'

'You…' hissed Nasir.

Jonas clapped his hands together. 'I was honoured to have been a part of this.'

'I knew that you were a disbanded, broken group by Jonas here drawing what was left of you out into the open. You make for such a pitiful collection. But now…' De Rainault raised his arms. 'You are all back together thanks to me.'

'You may regret that, Sheriff,' said Robin.

Jonas reached into a purse at his waist and threw a handful of wooden coins at the feet of the outlaws. 'All that you're worth to the peasants you hold so dear.'

'You turned your back on them, so I'm told,' de Rainault said to Robin. 'The People's Champion who couldn't care less about them. How the tide has turned.'

Robin wouldn't be taunted. 'Where is my daughter?'

'She is with her mother,' came the Sheriff's reply. 'Actually *mothers*, if we include the surrogate. The leverage that ensured you played my little game and did my bidding. That's something the people will remember when this story is re-told. The wolfshead that was tamed,' gloated de Rainault.

'People won't believe it!' John exclaimed, but Robin knew that de Rainault would see to it that they were not around to offer an alternative version of events.

'Where are they?' Robin said through gritted teeth.

'Safe enough, if you agree to my terms.'

And what are your terms, Sheriff?' Robin asked.

'It's quite simple, really.' De Rainault walked around Robin and his men. 'You are to accept your fate and offer no resistance.'

'What do we get in return?' asked Robin.

'The chance to meet your child and say goodbye. She will not be harmed. In fact, through my benevolence, your child will grow up safely as a simple peasant, but with a family of my choosing.'

'What of Marion?'

'She is a member of the Church,' said de Rainault. 'I will return her to Halstead and she can end her days behind its walls. My brother will ensure the Abbess does not allow her to leave ever again, especially not on some apparent sabbatical.'

'May you rot in *jahannam*,' cursed Nasir as the Sheriff drew level with him.

'Something tells me you will get there first,' de Rainault said in his ear. 'Bertrand, settle them into their new accommodations.'

Into the square came a heavy prison wagon pulled by four horses. Bertrand motioned for Will Scarlet to lead the outlaws to the cramped-looking cage.

'Er, I'm not sure we'll fit,' Tuck ventured, as they were forced in at sword point. John promised, once again, that he would find a way to settle things with Scarlet as the barred wooden door was shut.

'Just a moment!' called de Rainault. 'That man there, he should be in the wagon as well!'

Bertrand eyed the Sheriff suspiciously. Scarlet was one of his men now, and as such, he was vouching for him. The fact that they even had the outlaws as prisoners should be all the proof that was needed as to where his loyalties lay. Nevertheless, de Rainault insisted that the wagon door be checked.

'Do you doubt your word, my Lord?' Bertrand asked.

'Not yours, no,' declared the Sheriff. 'But I do doubt Scarlet's.'

With a shrug, Bertrand tried the door to prove it was locked. It was now Robin's turn to speak up.

'De Rainault, you said I could say goodbye.'

'And I am a man of my word,' the Sheriff replied as Esther, carrying a baby, and with Marion by her side, appeared out of the crowd. As they reached the wagon, the outlaws gave Robin his space.

'I didn't know what de Rainault had planned,' said Marion, with tears flowing down her face.

'I know,' he assured her gently.

Composing herself, Marion smiled at Esther, who moved forward so that Robin could properly see his daughter for the first time.

'Meet Robyn of Sherwood,' Marion said.

'Oh, my child… Thank you Marion,' said Robin in a whisper. His head was in a whirlwind as he gazed upon his daughter for the first time. He reached out to touch Robyn's forehead but his arm was clouted away by Jonas.

'That's enough!' the steward called, clearly looking to make his mark as the Sheriff's new pet. Robin glared at him, swearing vengeance under his breath.

'I am keen to get underway,' de Rainault said. 'Bertrand!'

Bertrand ordered his men to pull the women away from the cart but Marion was able to grab Robin's hand and they looked at each other with an intensity that connected them in a moment of understanding. It was, for those few seconds, as if the years and the anguish had been wiped clean away.

'Where there's a Will…' she whispered, as finally the mercenaries hauled her, Esther and Robyn to a waiting cart.

As they began to move out, all Robin himself could do was sink back into the moving cell. John put his hand on Robin's shoulder.

'Are you alright?' he asked gently.

'It's a lot to take in,' Robin confessed, staring out at the town's walls then upwards as they passed through the gates.

'I never imagined we would have the threat of one of our own children's safety hanging over us. It's different somehow.'

'Oh, it's different alright, John. I love every one of you as brothers. My daughter… she's so innocent, so vulnerable.'

'She will have our protection. Always,' said Nasir.

'We're not done for,' John said. 'We never are.'

'We will get out of this won't we?' Much was worried they'd end up in the dungeons in Nottingham Castle. He hated it there, was utterly terrified of it.

'Of course we will,' soothed Robin.

'How?' Much's eyes were forming tears.

'Oh, well there's this for a start.' Robin smiled as he opened his fist. 'It's been sticking in my palm ever since Marion passed it to me. A gift from Will.'

It was the key to the wagon's door.

'Scarlet!! I knew it! I knew it all along!' said John, his face beaming. 'He would never betray us!'

Robin stretched out his other hand, to apologise to Tuck, and it was clasped firmly by the Friar. 'I'm sorry, Tuck,' he said, 'I'm sorry to you all. I've been asleep too long. But now… we fight back!'

The simple but heartfelt apology was warmly accepted it, and with it there was an unspoken re-kindling of the bond of friendship between them all. Not only that, but a strengthening of the cause to fight the oppression that united them. There was a long way to go yet, but Robin had taken the first definitive step to make things right again.

***

The convoy of riders and wagons had crossed a wide clearing to come upon the edge of a wood, more densely packed with trees than any similar landscape since leaving Barnsley some hours before. At de Rainault's instigation they came to a halt.

'Do you know what that is?' he asked Bertrand, motioning with a gloved hand, finger pointing.

'More forest, what of it?' sighed Bertrand, moving his horse so he was next to the Sheriff.

'Ah yes, but not just any forest,' the Sheriff informed him. That is Sherwood. And here in this clearing is the perfect place to end this little tour.'

'Sherwood,' murmured Bertrand, then nodding towards the wagon that caged Robin and the outlaws. 'His forest.'

'As *he* sees it. It is the King's, of course. But that seems not to matter to the likes of him. I want them to see how near, and yet how far, they are to their beloved greenwood.'

'It makes little difference to me where you conclude our business. I just want to get out of this wretched weather,' replied Bertrand. 'But I would like to know how you intend to settle your debt if we are not going to Nottingham.'

'I can assure you that payment is forthcoming. You will be handsomely rewarded for your involvement in bringing Robin Hood to justice.'

Right on cue, a large detachment of the Sheriff's soldiers, fresh from the castle, rode into the clearing.

'Who are these men, my Lord?'

'Let's say they are additional security, Bertrand.' Then to Jonas: 'Lytham, assign your men.'

The new arrivals surrounded the mercenaries and, feeling the situation slipping from his control, Bertrand was distracted enough to not see de Rainault pull his dagger from under his purple cloak until it was too late. He felt the blade pierce his side, and he cried out in agony. The Sheriff had found a weak spot in his armour, the knife deep under his ribs.

'Mouchard…' he gasped, then louder, '*Mouchard!* We are betrayed!'

Mouchard urged his horse to gallop over to his leader, who was frantically attempting to unsheath his sword. Mouchard saw de Rainault lean in to Bertrand again and grab the dagger, twisting it before pulling it out. Bertand cried out again as the blood gushed over his legs and he slipped from his saddle onto the ground.

Mouchard was torn for a split second between dismounting to tend to his patron or order his men to attack the soldiers. But the decision was made for him as the double-crossing Sheriff of Nottingham gave the signal to Jonas to launch the offensive.

***

'He certainly hasn't changed,' Robin said of the Sheriff as fighting erupted all around them.

'Time to act, then,' agreed John.

Robin shifted positions, moving to where he could get the key into the lock of the wagon's door. As he did, one of Jonas' soldiers rode up close and they heard something land on the roof. Within a matter of seconds, the wagon was alight!

With the flames spreading quickly, Robin could feel the intense heat of the fire and to his horror, realised that flames were fusing the lock and key together. 'John get over here and get this door free!' he shouted.

But John, stuck as he was in the small space behind Tuck, was in no position to do anything.

'The fire's burning through the wood!' Much cried. 'If you're going to do something, Robin, do it!'

If ever Robin had needed all his strength it was now, as he began to frantically kick at the door. But the door was made to not be kicked out so easily, so calming himself and closing his eyes, Robin focused his mind. 'Herne, Lord of the Trees, hear me!'

Robin felt a surge of strength flow through him and with a fresh series of kicks, he had smashed the door open. As they scrambled out, the outlaws, taking huge gulps of fresh air, saw the prison cart finally engulfed in a ball of fire.

With carnage raging all around them, if they were to live, they needed to fight. As the outlaws grabbed whatever weapons they could, Robin needed to get to Marion.

Taking cover behind their wagon, Esther was shielding Robyn whilst Marion picked up a fallen cross bow and took aim at an advancing man-at-arms, only to see him tackled to the ground by Robyn's father. As he emerged from the struggle to flash a smile at her, Marion fired her bolt and another soldier, who had been trying to sneak up on Robin, fell to the ground.

If he had expected a hero's return, then Robin was disappointed as Marion shouted at him to pick up a sword and fight!

In the midst of the skirmish, unused to a sword, Little John swung the weapon only to have the blow parried by another blade that was wielded in a more expert fashion. 'You could have killed me,' cried Scarlet.

'Sorry,' replied John ruefully. 'You looked like a soldier.'

'You of all people should know that looks can be deceiving,' Scarlet replied.

With a smile, John agreed wholeheartedly with his friend, as side by side, they charged into the melee.

Jonas was immediately upon them, ensuring he was within sight of his master. To kill two of the outlaws would indeed put him in good stead. He was aware that his predecessor, Sir Guy of Gisburne, hadn't managed that small task.

Will was surprised at the ferocity of Jonas' attack. The steward may have been wiry, but he was younger and faster and dodged most of Will's stabs and thrusts. Another soldier appeared to help but was easily beaten down by John, using his forehead to make the final blow. The soldier crashed to the ground, unconscious, as John shook his shaggy mane and darted towards a group of mercenaries overpowering Much.

Marion stayed as close to Esther and Robyn as she could, killing two soldiers and injuring one of Mouchard's men as they came too near.

Esther screamed as an arrow fixed itself into the wagon just above her head. Marion looked outwards and saw Mouchard himself mounting a second arrow. She was quickly aiming her crossbow now and a bolt embedded deep into Mouchard's shoulder. He dropped the bow, the arrow falling aimlessly, and he himself rolled to the ground in agony.

De Rainault had moved to the edge of Sherwood, out of harm's way, just as a coward would do. Robin had seen him retreat but knew the man wouldn't dare venture into the forest alone. If anything, it meant that Robin could be assured the Sheriff wouldn't sneak away during the fight.

Will was still battling one on one with Jonas and seemed to be losing so Robin dashed over to help. Will nodded once at Robin in acknowledgement as they cornered Jonas against the wagon.

'Give up now,' Robin cried. 'You're not wanted here in Sherwood. You're an interloper. Now call your men off or we will end your life now.'

Jonas went to spit some expletive but decided against it, instead shouting out to the soldiers to cease the fight.

'You've still lost!' Jonas said. 'You may have been King of Sherwood once but you're its history now.'

'And who is there in its place, Jonas?' asked Robin. 'You?'

'Why not? I fought in the Holy Lands, I can live with what the forest gives me.'

'Yeah, but for how long? You wouldn't last a day. Looks like you're still just a kid,' added Will. 'It's you that has lost.'

'Even your Sheriff cowers by the trees,' said Robin.

'Not for long. Look.'

Robin turned to see what Will meant and saw a badly injured Bertrand pushing de Rainault forward. The surviving mercenaries wanted his blood. De Rainault's response was to remark on the deep looking wound that he had inflicted on their leader.

'I'll live. Unlike you,' Bertrand said. 'You want me to kill him now, Hood?'

A rumble of approval was abruptly silenced by Robin, but Bertrand understood. 'You want the honour for yourself.'

Now the mercenaries were jeering and Scarlet, John, Much and Nasir were also protesting. Bertrand held up his hand to calm his men as Robin turned to Tuck, but the Friar looked to Marion.

'After everything he's done, it's no more than he deserves,' she said.

'But?' Robin asked, already sensing the answer.

'It would be very easy. Sometimes there must be a penance to pay.'

'There it is, then,' Robin declared. 'You've been sentenced, Sheriff. Sentenced to live with the knowledge that you failed. Sentenced to live with the knowledge that Sherwood is once again mine.'

Bertrand gave a guffaw as raucous as his wound would allow. 'After all that, you would let him live!'

'Life, for people like him, can sometimes be more agonising than the release of death,' Robin said. 'Bertrand, I grant you and your men safe passage out of Sherwood.'

'You are too trusting.'

'No, Bertrand,' Will said. 'This is on the condition that you never return. If you do, you ain't leaving again.'

'Mouchard,' called Bertrand. 'One of your mercenaries has become turnabout. Seems he has returned to his old ways.'

Mouchard staggered to them, blood congealing around the bolt in his shoulder.

'Will Scarlet is free. As are we all,' declared Robin,

'I like you, outlaw!' Bertrand exclaimed with a hearty laugh. 'Mouchard, my crossbow and my horse.' As he mounted up, he gave Robin a nod. 'I accept your terms,' he said. 'All but one.'

Before anyone could stop him, Bertrand had fired his crossbow; sending a bolt straight into the Sheriff's chest, who, with a surprised gasp, collapsed onto the ground.

Robin was furious. Bertrand though was unapologetic.

'You've no idea what you've done,' said Robin.

'Oh, I think I do,' Bertrand replied. '*Au revoir*, Robin Hood!' And with that, he led his men away at a gallop.

The outlaws looked at each other and at the retreating forms of Bertrand, Mouchard and the other giants, then they looked down at De Rainault.

'Help him!' Jonas called. 'I demand you help him!'

Much stepped forward, tentative, unsure. 'Should we, Robin?'

The surviving soldiers were tending their own wounds, as convinced as Robin was of the Sheriff's outcome.

'Perhaps this is a new chapter,' Robin said. 'Perhaps this is meant to be. One of us was always likely to out-survive the other. It could have been either of us.' He looked down at the Sheriff. 'I saved your life, Robert de Rainault. It seems your allies did not share the same sentiment. Remember that for the time you had left. Your greatest enemy showed you compassion.'

'I'll… I'll kill you… wolfshead…' the Sheriff gasped, before slumping to the ground, lifeless.

***

The sun cast long shadows through the trees as Robin and his friends sat around the campfire Much was tending to.

There was a pall of sadness that was hindered by the knowledge that soon little Robyn would be leaving with her new parents. It seemed a lifetime ago that they used to play and wrestle, sing bawdy songs and recount their exploits of the day, Scarlet usually embellishing specific details, mainly where he had been the ringleader in a particularly daring escape.

Robin was cradling his daughter in his arms, not breaking his gaze from her precious features. Her freckles displaying her mother's characteristics, she looked like Marion for sure, auburn locks already turning to curls and her blue eyes alert and taking in everything around them. Esther stared at him, not breaking her gaze. It had taken Tuck to convince her at great length that Robin and Marion needed this special time with their daughter before she and Geoffrey took her back to Wellow for good.

'This is our home,' Robin said to his little girl, 'but it's not safe for you. You're the most beautiful thing in the whole of Sherwood and you deserve a far better life than we can ever give you.'

Marion moved in close to him and put an arm around his waist.

He'd missed her touch, the way she looked at him and the scent of her hair and he wanted nothing more for the three of them to never be apart. But it could never be: their enemies could exploit Robyn as a weakness and she would always be in danger. He was dreading the next few moments.

'She will be just fine,' Marion said, choking back the tears that were forming. She had already given up Robyn and so this was just something she had gotten used to. Her time in Halstead had shown her ways to cope but she felt her control crumbling. No. She had to be strong for all three of them. She sighed as Robin snaked his own arm around her small waist and Robyn nestled between them both. 'Come on. We have to do this.'

'A few moments more, please…'

Robin dared not blink, not wanting to lose even a split second of seeing his daughter for one last time. As Marion gently took their child, he knew that this was the only way.

'We can't delay. It's getting dark,' Marion said.

Together, Robin and Marion walked over to where Esther and Geoffrey were waiting by their wagon. As they took Robyn from Marion's arms, Geoffrey was genuine in his sentiment. He and Esther had already fallen in love with little Robyn and gave his word she would be cared for as if she were their very own.

'When she is older, when the time is right, we will tell her of her heritage. Who her father was and how he always looked out for us, even if we weren't all from Sherwood.'

'If you do, make sure she is safe. Any indication that she is ours may prove to be dangerous for her.'

'I understand, Robin.'

'Where will you go?' Robin asked, but Marion touched his arm.

'We're not going back to Wellow. There is a risk that the Sheriff's successor might be told that's where we came from.'

'We promise we will send word as soon as we're settled,' Esther added.

'No, you can't,' said Marion sadly. 'As hard as this is, you can't. The only way we can protect her is by not knowing where she is. You'd better go, before I change my mind.'

Marion pulled Robin away and back to the circle, hiding her sobs from anyone who was watching, which was everybody.

'Marion,' Tuck began. 'Little Flower…'

She buried her face in Tuck's broad chest as Robin sank to the ferny floor, the temptation of drink calling to him to wipe this memory from his mind. But they weren't in Wickham anymore, they were back in Sherwood. They were home.

***

John saw Nasir sitting on a log some distance away from the group, who had occasionally been looking at Robin and Marion and their daughter, and headed towards him.

'Quieter than usual, Nas?' John noted as he sat next to his friend. Nasir raised an eyebrow and took another glance at the baby who by now was heading away from them with her new parents. 'That must be tough for Robin and Marion.'

Nasir nodded solemnly and looked at his boots. 'It is. I know.'

John opened his mouth to speak then paused, closed it, opened it again, decided against saying anything and stood instead. He was about to return to the fire but hesitated once more. 'What do you mean?'

'I mean I know. It is hard to give up your children. It is something that burns away at me every day.'

'Burns away?' John sat back down. The log wobbled. 'Have you got..?' The question lingered in the air between the two men. Nasir eventually nodded.

'I do not speak of them because it pains me to do so.' Nasir shifted in his seat, clearly uncomfortable and unused to talking so openly in this way. But he trusted John.

'Of all the years I've known you, it never occurred to me you were a father.' It was something none of them had ever contemplated simply because Nasir was intensely private.

'Husband, father,' Nasir replied, forlornly. 'Robin and Marion, they should cherish their child. But I know they cannot. Must not. Like them, I had to give mine up for their own safety. Yet they are fortunate they still have each other.'

'Aye, lad,' the giant agreed, thinking of Meg and his own decision to return to Sherwood. He looked over to Scarlet who was gesticulating animatedly as he told stories to young Much of his time with Mouchard. Scarlet's was the saddest story of all: his wife raped and murdered by Normans, forever filling his heart with anger.

But they had each other again now, all of them. Time would be a healer and trust, although already earnt through their time together even after Loxley had been killed, would be solid once more. John knew it, could feel it. Perhaps it was Herne's spirit, guiding them together once more, for Robin seemed passionate again, the fight for the oppressed driving him, driving all of them, onwards just like the old days. But there would always be time for reflection, because nothing was ever forgotten.

'Nasir, I'm sorry,' John breathed, placing a large hand on his friend's shoulder.

'It is what it is. It is not for changing.' Nasir shrugged off the affection and stood. 'Come. I cook now. I have *not* missed Tuck's attempts.' Nasir gave a flash of a smile and strode off.

John gave a loud guffaw and joined him.

***

The next morning, they returned to Wickham.

Edward was surprised but overjoyed to welcome them all back and for his part, Robin was keen to assure the head man that he had no plans to move back into the barn.

Edward was relieved. 'Cate was always complaining that you soured Audrey's milk.'

Robin looked at him, confused.

'Cate, our old milk maid. Audrey is her cow.'

Robin burst out laughing and hugged Edward. 'It never occurred to me either of them had names! But please reassure both ladies I shan't be darkening their door again!'

'They will be glad to hear it.'

***

John Little as big and overbearing and as fierce as he was, paused outside his own home, nervous as to what he would find.

'I know you're out there, John,' called Meg from within. 'I can hear you grinding your teeth.'

John shook his head and pushed open the door, stunned to see that Meg was sat on the bed, holding the very box he had come to retrieve.

'I'm sorry,' he said. 'I thought I'd just slip in and get it and then be gone. Out of your life.'

'But then we wouldn't see each other,' Meg replied softly.

'Isn't that what you want?' John asked.

'I'm here John. Here because I do want to see you,' she replied.

'Me too,' said John.

'I know you have things you need to do. But can we talk later?'

'Talk?' John asked.

'Is such a brave man afraid of a few words?' Meg replied.

'No. Talk,' said John with a smile. 'I'd like that… Very much.'

As she returned his smile, Meg handed him the box. He needed to get it to Robin.

***

The flaming arrow sped through the sky and dropped into the water with a hiss. A second one followed.

Robin and Marion looked out onto the rippling surface of the lake as the sun disappeared, the forest entering twilight. They lowered their long bows.

'For our daughter, for all that she'll be. She will live in our hearts,' said Marion softly. 'From this moment, we can never mention her.'

'We have done the right thing, haven't we?' asked Robin. The doubt, he feared, would always remain with him.

'She'll be safe. Our silence will not be our pain, it will be our love for her, unbroken and enduring,' Marion replied.

He kissed her forehead and they strode arm in arm away from the lake.

'What will you do now, Sister Marion?'

'I can't go back to Halstead, that's for sure.'

Robin nodded. 'Abbot Hugo is likely already out for revenge.'

'Do you think he's really dead?'

'The Sheriff?' Robin shook his blonde head. 'I don't know. I hope so. I want him to be. It would make things easier.'

'And if he's not?'

'Then the fight goes on, until whoever does succeed him will be a noble and just ruler. Until then…'

Marion stopped walking just shy of the camp and Robin turned to face her. 'It won't ever end, though, will it?'

'Perhaps one day,' Robin sighed.

'Geoffrey said he'd tell our daughter all about us when the time is right. We'll be just stories to her.'

'Yes. We will.'

'But what if she comes looking? Comes to Sherwood one day as a young woman? What if the stories Geoffrey tells her make her want to—'

'Pick up a longbow?' Robin laughed gently. 'That would indeed be a sight, her returning to claim her birthright. She'd show us a thing or two, eh, our Robyn of Sherwood? But…'

'What?' Marion replied, looking up into his eyes that seemed older, more seasoned… more wary perhaps. 'What is it?'

'You never answered my question, Sister Marion.' Robin took a deep breath. 'Do you love me?'

'Why, yes, of course I do, Robin. But that wasn't your question.'

'No. It wasn't.'

'I can't go back to Halstead and it's not because of any revenge the Abbot might decide to bestow upon me.'

'Then why, Sister?'

'Do I have to say it?' Marion responded.

'I need to know,' said Robin.

'Very well,' Marion replied gently. 'Because a life can't be lived without heartbreak and I can't go back because I love you. I am not Sister Marion of Halstead, but Marion of Sherwood. And we will not be parted again. I lost more than I thought I ever could and I cannot bear to be away from you one moment longer.'

***

The riders came thundering to a halt in the clearing outside Sherwood. The scene that greeted them was one of desolation and death, as they looked upon the burnt-out prison wagon and the bodies that were strewn across the ground.

Flynn, the captain of the men-at-arms turned to the Abbot Hugo. 'What has happened here?'

'My brother's gamble,' the Abbot replied, sombrely. 'One which he appears to have finally lost.'

They dismounted. The Abbot gave orders for the dead to be attended to, whilst he walked over to the crumpled form of his brother. On reaching the body, he gently rolled the Sheriff over.

'Robert,' Hugo said with a sigh. 'Sleeping dogs, brother. I did try to warn you.'

He was about to say a final prayer when, very weakly, the Sheriff called his name.

It took Hugo a moment to take in what had happened but then he checked his brother's armour and called out for Flynn, who came running over.

'Send men to the nearest village and get a cart,' Hugo ordered.

'Is my Lord Sheriff..?' Flynn didn't dare finish the sentence.

Hugo nodded. 'A hardened leather plate under his chain mail. Where is that cretin Jonas?'

'He is not among the dead, Your Holiness.'

'No matter.' Hugo placed a hand on the Sheriff's shoulder. 'You have luck that simply doesn't run out, brother.'

'How is it that he survived?'

'The bolt got through it but the wound isn't deep. He's lost a lot of blood.'

Flynn was now up and ordering his men to go quickly as the Abbot had commanded.

Hugo turned his attention back to his brother.

'Hugo,' Robert de Rainault whispered weakly. 'Get me back to Nottingham.'

Hugo again shouted at the Captain to make haste with the cart they needed.

The Lord High Sheriff of Nottingham was alive!

EPILOGUE

Sherwood Forest seemed to sigh with contentment as Robin held court amongst the trees.

It was a balmy night, the warmest it had been this year. Before them, in the middle of their circle, was the thin wooden casket John had brought back from Wickham.

'You should prepare yourself,' John has said as he'd lain it down.

Robin stared at it, then looked around at his companions.

'What have I done?' he whispered.

'You weren't yourself, Robin,' Marion said. 'Perhaps none of us were. Open it.'

Robin shuffled forward on his knees, grabbed the lid of the box and took a deep breath. Gently, and with trepidation, he went to open it but the lid was firm so he tugged at it hard. As it finally came loose in his hands, he staggered back.

They all staggered back.

A blinding white light shot up, out from the box and as it subsided and despite John's warning, nothing could have prepared them for what they saw within.

For there was Albion, shining bright and whole again.

In shock, Robin took his sword in his hand and raised it up, the daylight glinting from the blade. 'Herne protect us,' he said aloud as the outlaws and Edward echoed him.

'Look!' Much cried. 'At the edge of the forest!'

They turned to see Herne, the great Lord of the Trees, his arms raised up in blessing, and heard his words on the wind.

'You are the hooded man, my arrow and my sword. So must it be, Robin 'i' the hood!'

As the wind blew, a flash of lightning streaked across the sky and Herne was gone. He had welcomed them all home, welcomed his son back.

Robin turned to his friends: John, Will, Tuck, Nasir, Much, Edward and Marion, most of all Marion. He sheathed Albion in its rightful place against his thigh and for the first time in a long time that he could remember, the thunder clouds parted and blue sky appeared.

A beam of warm sunlight lit up the ground around them.

Our friends who died will never die of hunger, be tortured or in the dark be chained. They are with us in Sherwood and they remain forever with us.

Because they are free.

What was lost was now found and the legend and the legacy of Robin of Sherwood was never to be doubted again.